THE
BENEFICIARIES

Also by Pamela Street:

The Timeless Moment

THE BENEFICIARIES

by

Pamela Street

ST. MARTIN'S PRESS
NEW YORK

THE BENEFICIARIES. Copyright © 1989 by Pamela Street. All rights reserved. Printed in the United States of America. No part of this book may be used or reproduced in any manner whatsoever without written permission except in the case of brief quotations embodied in critical articles or reviews. For information, address St. Martin's Press, 175 Fifth Avenue, New York, N.Y. 10010.

Library of Congress Cataloging-in-Publication Data

Street, Pamela.
    The beneficiaries / Pamela Street.
        p.   cm.
    ISBN 0-312-03796-1
    I. Title.
    PR6037.T8175B46   1990
    823'.914—dc20   89-24163
                                                          CIP

First published in Great Britain by Robert Hale Limited.

First U.S. Edition

10 9 8 7 6 5 4 3 2 1

1

It was a damned silly will to have left, Joanna Lawson thought, as she sat listening to the executor, Mr Pemberton, going through its contents after the funeral was over. But then, she reflected, her late mother Lady Rayner had always been capricious, the more so as she grew older. Joanna would not really have been surprised at anything she did; and Gloria would certainly have never brooked any advice over the way she bequeathed her estate, either from the now retired Percy Pemberton or his associates in the firm of Pemberton Stubbs in Chancery Lane.

Holding her copy of the will which had arrived some days previously, Joanna took a few surreptitious glances at the other occupants seated in the drawing-room at Crane Lodge, Richmond. Apart from the elderly lawyer and the handsome younger one, Hugh Cory, whom he had brought with him, there were three other beneficiaries besides herself, whose faces bore extraordinarily different expressions.

On her right sat Bernard, Joanna's brother: fifty-four, fat and florid, his whole manner showing every sign of impatience and irritation. On Bernard's other side sat Mildred Treadgold, the Rayner family's one-time nannie, then governess – for Mildred had been well educated – who had stayed on after her charges had outgrown her services to become, at varying times, housekeeper, secretary and, after Sir Reginald Rayner's death, a long-suffering companion to his widow. Dear Mildred. Joanna was well aware that it was she who had then made it possible for her and Bernard to limit their filial duties to regular telephone calls and the odd visit. Today, wearing an unobtrusive navy crêpe two-piece, her greyish-white hair hanging thin and straight on either side of her pale, curiously child-like face, she looked as if she had found herself in a grown-up party at which she had no right to be.

On Joanna's left there sat far the most interesting of the little gathering, at least, so far as she was concerned. She had never seen a great deal of Herbert Fane, although she thought about him a lot. He was invariably charming and kind, gave her splendid presents at Christmas and on her birthday, but there was something about him which precluded any closer relationship. The first time that he had really registered with her was when she was a child and had been sent home early one afternoon from the day-school she was then attending because she had a headache. There was this curious, smartly dressed, good-looking man coming out of her mother's bedroom and she had wondered whether, perhaps, he was a doctor, for he had said, 'Ah, Joanna, I think it would be as well if you did not disturb your mother for a while. She is resting.'

Actually, Joanna had had no intention of disturbing Gloria, despite her headache. Gloria, with her exotic dragonfly beauty, had never been that kind of mother. Mildred was the person to go to for comfort and she had trotted along to the old nursery quarters in the west wing where she had found her, as expected, surrounded by sewing and newspapers and listening to a Brahms concerto on her wireless.

After being generally fussed over by Mildred and told to 'go and lie down, dear', Joanna had enquired, as she left the room, as to the exact identity of the visitor whom she had encountered on the front landing. To Joanna's surprise, Mildred had gone all pink and mumbled something about him being a friend of the family. Joanna could not understand how he could possibly have been that, for he never seemed to be around when her father was at home, but something warned her it was best not to pursue the matter.

It was not until Bernard came back from Harrow for the holidays that she decided to ask her brother for further information. Bernard was then sixteen and Joanna four years his junior. He was a big boy, heavy-jowled, slightly pompous, even in those days. Somehow, to Joanna, he had never been young. She recalled how he had looked at her in his knowing superior way and said, 'You're old enough to be told, I suppose. He's our mater's lover.

Herbert Fane. I call him H, but not to his face, of course. Ma calls him Bertie.'

Life had never seemed quite the same for Joanna after that. She became confused as to what a lover was. Bernard had insinuated it was someone not quite nice. Yet the man coming out of her mother's bedroom looked a pleasant enough character, even though he bore no resemblance to the one she invariably had in her mind's eye whenever they sang *There was a Lover and his Lass* at school. After all, Gloria was no lass, the strange visitor was middle-aged and Sir Reginald Rayner, recently knighted for his exploits in distant lands, was still alive.

During the rest of her teens, Joanna spent a lot of time wondering how much her father knew about Bertie Fane, this now elderly yet still distinguished-looking man, seated on her left, who appeared faintly out of place as he fingered his bow-tie and looked down at his incredibly well polished shoes. By the time she left school, Joanna had decided that her father must have been well aware of him and was, perhaps, relieved to feel that his wife had male companionship while he himself was going up the Nile or hacking his way through some South American jungle. It also occurred to Joanna that possibly the relationship between Gloria and Bertie had something other than sex which kept it going.

For Bertie was a dress-designer, not altogether in the Dior/Chanel class, but nevertheless that was his vocation and, as he grew older, so he designed for the older woman. Gloria was beautiful, she had a perfect figure, a passion for clothes and an insatiable desire for flattery. The two of them complemented each other very well. Joanna was aware that latterly they had not seen so much of each other, but whether this was simply due to advancing years or some deeper reason she had no idea.

Her present guarded contemplation of the man was suddenly brought to a halt by Mr Pemberton loudly clearing his throat and saying, 'It is extremely difficult to judge at this stage, but at a conservative estimate, it is my firm's opinion . . .' and here he made a brief sideways nod towards his younger colleague 'that the deceased will

9

have left something like two million, possibly more. This house, I believe, holds many treasures, relics brought back by the late Sir Reginald from his various explorations. Remember, of course, that Capital Transfer Tax will be heavy.'

There was silence, broken suddenly by Gloria's pekinese, Jason, yapping at the door and wanting to be let in.

'Once we have obtained probate,' Percy continued, when Jason, thanks to Mildred, had happily settled himself on a *chaise longue* at the end of the room, 'and this house and its effects have been sold and all the shares realised, everything gathered in, so to speak, a trust will be set up to be administered by myself and Mr Cory. With the aid of reliable financial advisers, the monies will be invested in gilt-edged stock and the income from this will be divided equally between you four beneficiaries.'

This time the silence was heavy, palpable, and when Percy Pemberton cleared his throat once again, it was as if a machine-gun had reverberated round the over-furnished room.

'And here we come to a rather delicate part of the will,' he eventually went on, 'which you will all no doubt have digested by now from the copies you have received, but I feel it as well to discuss it, especially as some of you may wish to raise questions.'

The old executor became a little hesitant now, as he regarded them all over the top of his half-moon spectacles. 'When one of you . . . er, passes on, although let us hope that such an occurrence is a long way hence,' he added hastily, 'the income will be redistributed equally between the remaining three beneficiaries, then . . . er, subsequently halved between two and . . . the last survivor will inherit the capital outright.'

Joanna felt her face redden, conscious that being the youngest, even if she *was* fifty, it might be logical to assume that she stood the best chance of winning the jackpot. Suddenly, she heard Bernard say, 'Mildred, I wonder if you could fetch a tray of glasses. I feel sure some of us could do with a drink.' He spoke in that sonorous order-giving voice of his which Joanna knew so well, making it obvious that he considered he was addressing an inferior, despite the fact that he and Mildred had been given equal status under the terms of Gloria Rayner's will.

But just as the poor woman, willing and flustered, rose to do Bernard's bidding, Mr Pemberton held up his hand. 'I have not quite finished, Mr Rayner. I would prefer no one to leave the room until I have. I should like to mention that, provided you all agree, it might be possible, under a Deed of Variation, to break the trust so that the capital be divided outright between the four of you now. This would, of course, depend on Counsel's opinion and each of you obtaining advice from your own solicitors. And, as I mentioned, it would be entirely dependent on you all being in perfect agreement.'

To Joanna, although she realised that ultimately, according to the law of averages, she stood more to lose by such a solution, it seemed an eminently sensible one. She felt the idea of four such disparate individuals wondering who was going to pop off first was not only ridiculous but somehow sinister. Why, it could be the plot for a play or a best-selling crime novel. She could even visualise a window display in the small bookshop she ran in the west country. But what couldn't she do with a lump sum now? She could expand her business, buy that dream cottage she had her eye on at Brimley End. Yet, even before Bernard spoke, she knew he would make difficulties. Her brother was that kind of man.

'I don't think I can agree to either of those possibilities, Mr Pemberton,' he said. 'I consider my mother's will to be quite extraordinary. I cannot imagine how anyone could have allowed it to be drawn up in such a way. I shall consult my own solicitors immediately.'

Which means, of course, Joanna said to herself, that Bernard is probably going to appeal, damn him. Hold everything up. This thing could drag on for ever.

Percy Pemberton nodded, gravely. He was a small white-haired man with a pleasant, courteous, old-fashioned manner. Although Lady Rayner's will might be giving him problems, Joanna felt he could well have had plenty of experience in dealing with dissatisfied legatees during his long and not undistinguished career. He gave the impression of having seen it all before: especially the greed, the jealousy which, sadly, was now manifesting itself all too plainly in the case of her brother. She noticed that Percy's assistant was simply looking anxious. It was a hot day and Hugh Cory ran a finger round the inside of his collar, as if both the room and its occupants were suddenly all too much for him. Joanna asked gently if perhaps another window could be opened. Mildred darted across towards one and began frantically tugging at the catch. With alacrity, the young lawyer rose to help her. Between them they at last managed to raise a sash and returned to their respective chairs, Mildred standing by hers, presumably wondering whether she would now be given permission to see to the drinks.

Percy Pemberton, possibly beginning to think that a whisky would not be such a bad idea after all and ignoring Bernard's last remark, said, 'Just one more point for now. It won't take long. May I assume that there would be no objection to Miss Treadgold, if she be so willing, making a start on the clearing up of Crane Lodge? She knows the house and I'm sure you will all agree that her services would be invaluable, for which the estate would make proper remuneration. And, of course, for insurance purposes alone, the house will have to be occupied pending the sale of the contents. Judging by the countless trunks and boxes I have seen in the attics and basement, the task will not be an easy one. Some sort of inventory will have to be made. Sir Reginald acquired so many unusual possessions which, understandably, Lady Rayner did not wish to dispose of after his death. There is such a wealth of . . . memorabilia at Crane Lodge. Of course, any of you would be entitled to call whenever you so wished and earmark such items as you might want to reserve at probate value.'

While Mildred still stood, smiling her acquiescence, and Bertie and Joanna made noises of appreciation and consent, Bernard burst out, rudely, 'You mean we have to *buy back* things like my mother's diamond necklace and earrings?'

This time even Percy Pemberton seemed discomfited.

Joanna felt infinitely sorry for him. He shouldn't have to be bothered with this job, she thought. He's too old. What a pity the other executor's dead. She was not at all saddened by her mother's death, nor was she hurt that Gloria had not seen fit to leave her any of her priceless jewellery. Unlike her mother, such possessions meant little to her. Yet she was suddenly overcome by an acute feeling of unease, even fear, which Percy Pemberton's next words did nothing to alleviate.

'Under the circumstances,' he replied, 'as Lady Rayner did not specify that any of her goods and chattels should go to any one person, I am afraid that is the procedure we shall have to adopt. I understand that the most valuable jewellery is already in the bank, and Mr Cory is arranging for the rest to be deposited there within the next few days.'

Bernard rose abruptly. He appeared to have forgotten about the drinks. 'I have to go,' he announced. 'As I said earlier, you will be hearing from my solicitors.' Then, turning to Joanna, he asked, 'Can I drive you back to central London? I take it you're going home tonight?'

'Thank you, yes,' she replied. 'I was rather hoping to catch the seven ten from Waterloo.'

He nodded and made for the door where he turned, raised an arm in a vague gesture of farewell to no one in particular, leaving his sister to shake hands all round and tell Mildred she would be in touch with her again very shortly.

Then she followed her brother out of the room, hoping that at least Percy Pemberton would now get a whisky.

2

Joanna found she was wrong in thinking that Bernard had forgotten about the drinks. Once in the car, he drove straight to the nearest pub.

'It seemed pointless to stay any longer at Crane Lodge. You and I have a lot to discuss,' he said, by way of explanation. 'You don't *have* to catch the seven ten, do you?'

'It's not imperative, but you must remember I'm a working woman. There'll be a lot to do tomorrow. I'm never too happy leaving the shop to one of the girls, who seem to come and go without ever knowing the difference between fact and fiction.'

'Yes, I dare say. But this is an emergency. If we handle the thing correctly, you could well not need to bother about working any more.'

She looked at him, incredulously. 'I happen to *like* what I'm doing, Bernard. The bookshop means everything to me now.'

He appeared either not to hear her remark or, what was more likely, she felt, had chosen to ignore it. But in any case, she realised the deeper meaning of her words would have been lost to him. The fact that she was a divorcée, who had never produced a family, yet had managed to make a life and living for herself which she had actually come to enjoy, was of no consequence to him compared with the overriding necessity of doing something quickly about trying to alter Gloria's will.

'Would you like to sit indoors or out and what would you like to drink?' he asked, as he held the car door open for her.

'I think I should like a gin and tonic and to sit over there by that mulberry tree,' she answered, beginning to walk towards it, while he disappeared to fetch their drinks.

'I nearly asked you to stay the night with us in Hampstead when we were speaking on the telephone earlier on,' he said, as he returned, 'but Felicity isn't at all well. That's why she wasn't at the funeral. Her nerves are

14

in a shocking state. It's the menopause. I can't imagine what she'll say when I tell her about Ma's jewellery.'

Joanna thought about Felicity as she watched him place their drinks on the rough wooden table between them, sit down heavily and take a large gulp of whisky. She could not remember her sister-in-law ever having been exactly well, nor an occasion when she was not complaining about something or other. The last thing Joanna wanted at that moment was to spend a night under her and Bernard's roof.

'Anyway, let's make the most of the time we have got,' Bernard went on. 'I consider it's quite unacceptable for you and me to be put in the same category as Mildred and H. You must see that. Here am I, a partner in a firm of well-known stockbrokers, being treated as if I'm not capable of handling my own money.' His face became redder. He took another large gulp of his drink and glowered at Joanna so that she wondered if, perhaps, apoplexy might carry him off before he ever received a penny.

She did her best to try and calm him down. 'But you heard what Percy Pemberton said. We could probably break the trust, have the money outright, provided we all agree. We could each have our dot, so speak, now.'

'*What?* Are you mad? I agree that the trust should be broken, but not that H and Mildred should have equal shares of the capital. What on earth is either of them going to do with maybe half or even a quarter of a million each? Look at their ages. It's just not on, Jo.' He banged his free hand down on the table, so that a young couple seated nearby looked up, startled.

'Mildred has family, nephews and nieces, I believe. Personally, I feel she's earned every penny of whatever may be coming to her. As for Bertie, well, he was pretty loyal to Ma over the years and she wasn't exactly easy. And he was awfully generous to us children.'

'That's as maybe. I think you've got a soft spot for the old boy. You mustn't let that kind of thing run away with you. Granted, I always reckoned Ma would leave him *something*, but not on this scale, not treat him like you and me. And he doesn't look short of a bob or two, does he? God, how I tried to find out what she was going to do about her will when Pa died, but she was so secretive. It was ridiculous him leaving her everything outright. I can't think why he never got around to altering his own will after they were first married, a man of his status, especially with the kind of risky life he led.'

'I don't think he thought much about death. He was all for life and living. I shall never forget how he helped me financially to set up the bookshop at the time of my divorce. As a matter of fact, Bertie wanted to do the same only my solicitors clamped down on it. They kept saying it would jeopardise my alimony.'

'Well, all I can say is I wish someone had got Ma to part with a bit of money while she was still alive. She's fairly snarled up the works now. Considering what she spent on her appearance, I'm surprised she's actually left as much as she has.'

'Maybe Bertie advised her on finance. After all, he was in business.'

'And her stockbroker son wasn't, I suppose? Oh, H is fly enough, all right. I wouldn't put anything past him.'

'Yet they didn't see quite so much of each other the last few years, did they?'

'No. I believe they must have had some kind of tiff. That's why I'm so surprised she's left him a quarter share in her estate or, rather, the income from it.'

'She must have wanted him to have it, surely? Otherwise, she'd have altered her will.'

'Not necessarily. It's the sort of thing a lot of people put off, like Pa. And she was getting so forgetful and eccentric towards the end.'

'Yes, although physically she was still pretty active, in spite of her heart trouble. The last time I saw her she was full of plans for going on a cruise.'

'What, with H?'

'No. With Mildred. What do you think she and Bertie might have quarrelled about?'

'I reckon he probably asked to marry her after Pa died and she refused.'

'Why would she do that?'

'My dear Jo. Ask yourself. The way of the world. She was Lady Rayner, wasn't she? She didn't want to be demoted to Mrs Fane.'

'Oh.'

Joanna, though invariably responsive to the finer sensibilities of others, was often blind to their less worthy characteristics. Being immune to snobbery herself, the idea that her mother might want to retain her title at all costs was something she had never considered; although now that Bernard had mentioned it, she could recall once having overheard Gloria ringing up some London shop and saying, 'This is *Lady* Rayner speaking,' as if she might have been royalty and, after putting down the receiver, turning to her daughter and remarking, 'The Lady bit usually does the trick. Otherwise one might have to wait ages.'

'Another drink, Jo?' Suddenly, she became aware that Bernard was standing, his glass empty. Her own was still half full.

'No thanks.' She sat, idly watching the scene before her as she waited for him to come back, a small fair pleasant-faced woman, but by no means endowed with her late mother's striking beauty; only in the large eyes, perhaps, was there a resemblance, but whereas Gloria's were icy blue, Joanna's were warm and friendly.

'I wouldn't have minded so much,' Bernard started up again, as soon as he returned with another double whisky, 'if Gloria had thought of George.' George was Felicity's son by her first marriage, whom Bernard had adopted, albeit reluctantly. He was a pale spindly boy who aroused Joanna's compassion on the rare occasions when she saw him. It was the first time she had ever heard her brother express much interest in the child.

'But it wasn't as if George was Gloria's own grandson,' she replied.

'No. But I've taken on full legal responsibility for him, haven't I? School fees. The lot. That shyster, Felicity's first husband, simply ducked out. Ma could have saved a hell of a lot of Capital Transfer Tax if she'd only settled money on the boy before she died. The very least she could have done was to leave something in trust for him in her will. Now, that *would* have been sensible.'

'I suppose she thought that she just had four people in her life with whom she felt . . . reasonably connected, and the simplest thing to do would be to give them a quarter share each. I can understand it, in a way.'

'Well, I can't. I shall try to get an appointment with Freddie Hetherington, my solicitor, tomorrow.'

'I can't see that you have grounds for an appeal, Bernard.'

'I mean to find out. Freddie's pretty clued up.' He finished his second drink quickly and looked at his watch. 'I'm afraid you've missed the seven ten, old girl. What'll you do for a meal? I'd like to offer to take you out, but Felicity . . . you understand . . .'

Joanna understood only too well. In any case, she had no desire to listen to Bernard going on about wills and trusts for the rest of the evening. She picked up her bag. 'Don't worry. I'll get a sandwich in the buffet while I wait for the later train.'

He drove, with impatience, back to central London, occasionally muttering expletives when they were held up by traffic lights or a car in front, regretting, more than once, that he had chosen to cross the Thames at Putney rather than carry on south of the river.

'I'll let you know what transpires with Hetherington,' he said, as he put her down at the station.

She was worried that he seemed to take it for granted that she would support him in what he was about to do and felt she must make it plain that she did not approve. As he leant over and opened the car door for her, she said, quietly, 'Bernard, you must do as you think fit. Personally, I'd prefer to leave everything in Pemberton's hands. If we can each have some capital now, so much the better, but as for any other attempt to alter Gloria's will, I'm against it.'

He shook his head. 'Poor old Jo. It's a pity you don't try to look after Number One a bit more. You don't even want your brother to act on your behalf, do you? Anyway, we'll be in touch.'

On the way home she sat back with her eyes closed, going over the events of the day. The heat, the rhythmic movement of the train, the extra gin and tonic which she had decided to treat herself to along with a ham sandwich at the buffet, all combined to send her into a lethargic, almost dream-like state through which Percy Pemberton, Hugh Cory, Mildred, Bertie and Bernard flitted in and out, wagging their heads, saying this, suggesting that. Even the mourners at the funeral seemed to come into the picture at times: Gloria's neighbours, the Jamiesons, the Collets, Mrs Bradley and General Fisk, the local bank manager, the gardener and the daily help – good heavens, she thought, surely those two should have been remembered in the will – and lastly, Dr Merton, who had been called in by Mildred the day she found her employer dead in bed when she had gone in with Gloria's morning tea.

Of course, it wasn't exactly unexpected, Joanna thought. Gloria had been on digoxin for ages, told to ease up and avoid stressful situations. All the same, it must have been ghastly for poor Mildred. Death was always a shock. It was so final when it came. Joanna found it hard to imagine that she herself would soon have no more ties with Crane Lodge, the large, rambling, unattractive Victorian edifice which, nevertheless, she had always thought of as home. She wondered where Mildred would go when she had done all the sorting and the place had been sold. It would be good to think of her happily settled in some pleasant house or flat of her own, nice to know she would have the wherewithal to buy it.

Joanna wondered whether, perhaps, she ought to write to Percy Pemberton at once, confirm how she felt about his proposed Deed of Variation to the will, irrespective of what Bernard was getting up to. Surely there was no need to obtain the approval of her own solicitor as the old executor had advised. She began composing a letter in her mind and then thought better of it. She was always a bit apt to rush her fences. It would be nice to talk the whole matter over with Sam Foster, the man with whom she had had a stop-go relationship for many years now. Then she decided against this also, at least for the time being. Sam was 'funny' about money. She had never entirely forgiven him for his attitude when she was going through her divorce.

The train sped on. Exhausted, Joanna slept her way through Woking, Basingstoke and Salisbury, mercifully waking just before Templecombe, where she got out and staggered to her waiting car.

3

Bertie Fane let himself into his house at Strand-on-the-Green and extracted an envelope – postmarked SW14 – from his letter-box. He knew who it was from, but he did not open it at once. Instead, he went into his specially designed kitchen, opened the back door and called 'Felix'. Immediately, a large black tom skittered down from an old apple tree and came running towards him, where it wound itself round his legs, purring loudly.

Bertie went back inside, opened a tin of cat food, put it into a special earthenware bowl and placed it on the porch. Felix was never fed indoors. Bertie, with the help of a Mrs Pardoe, kept his home, like himself, in immaculate order at all times. Yet the place was never just a show piece. With the same flair which he had once used to dress his various 'ladies', especially Gloria, he had managed to combine baroque, genuine antique, reproduction and selected modern furniture and pictures to give an overall air of casual friendly elegance.

He was not a rich man, at least, not nearly as rich as Bernard had intimated to Joanna. He had sold his business at a bad time during a bout of acute depression, something which had become more frequent as the years caught up with him. But whereas this had been a nebulous kind of malady, lately he had been troubled by certain physical symptoms, about which he was not only depressed but scared. The thought of all the various afflictions attendant on old age started to haunt him. He knew the unopened letter was from his doctor concerning something of this sort, that the news would be either good or bad, and he was sure that it would be the latter. He found he was right.

When Bertie at last summoned up courage to read it, the most pertinent lines seemed to spring out at him, almost as if they had been printed in darker type: *It will be necessary for Mr Smithson to operate as soon as possible . . .*

He sat quite still, staring out across the Thames. The last rays of the September sun flecked the water with gold, making it look like shot silk: but this evening its beauty failed to register with him. What light there was seemed strange and metallic. It was always the same when his depression deepened. There was a darkness which came from within, dulling his senses, dulling the whole world around him.

He had first noticed a transitory numbness in his left foot some weeks ago when he was getting out of bed. He had supposed it was due to the way he had been lying and thought nothing more of it. Then it returned one evening when he was sitting in his drawing-room, just as now, looking out of the window at his favourite view. On attempting to rise, he had been forced to wait a few moments for ordinary feeling to return. The possibility that he might be going to have a stroke came instantly to mind. He saw his G.P. the following day.

He thought Sullivan was cagey after giving him a thorough examination in his consulting-rooms. He said he would like Bertie to see a man in Harley Street, 'just to be on the safe side,' he had added. The fact that the appointment with a Mr Smithson was fixed up so quickly seemed ominous, the more so when Bertie was asked by him to return to a nearby clinic the following day for a series of tests. And now, according to the letter he held in his hand, it appeared that a small growth had been discovered 'in an area of the brain,' Sullivan wrote, 'where removal will be easy, after which there is every chance of a speedy and entirely successful recovery.' In the final paragraph, he proposed that Bertie should enter hospital the following Monday.

He sat for a long while still staring out of the window, the letter lying on a small table beside him. He did not share Sullivan's optimism. Supposing the operation was not successful? Supposing it left him brain-damaged? Confined to a hospital for incurables? What about expense? He might today have learned that he had 'expectations', but a malady such as his could cost hundreds, even thousands a week. Please God he would be able to suffer it privately. The thought of being ill in a public ward appalled him. He knew his medical insurance would cover the cost of the operation but, whatever happened, he would need after-care, perhaps *ad infinitum*. Besides, since his problems over depression, the authorities seemed to think he was more of a risk. They hadn't been quite so good about handing out reimbursement. Insurers did not take kindly to mental cases.

It occurred to him that perhaps there was a connection between his nervous illness and the physical one which had just been diagnosed. Maybe the growth had been coming on a long time, even though Sullivan stressed it was so small. One never really knew about these things. Doctors didn't know all that, either. He remembered once telling Gloria, as a small joke, that it was just *because* they knew so little that they were always having to *practise*. Thank God for her legacy, whichever way it was handled. He hadn't been expecting anything and, if it were not for this particular blow, he believed he might have made some generous gesture with his share in favour of someone else. But now, with the news he had just received . . .

His mind went back to when he had first known Gloria. So incredibly beautiful she had been. He could see her now as she walked into his salon one day, saying she wanted some outfits made for Ascot. He had had far richer and more distinguished clients on his books at that time, but none was a patch on Mrs Gloria Rayner, as she was then. She had appealed to his aesthetic senses. He could remember the thrill it gave him just to hold up a swatch of material against her slim, exquisitely proportioned body. It had never entered his head that she would suddenly ask him to join the party in which she was going to Ascot, that he was, in fact, to be her escort because her husband was abroad.

They had not become lovers for quite a while and, even then, it had never been a passionate affair. As Joanna had rightly suspected, their relationship was based on other things. They were simply two lonely people who had found that each, however unintentionally, had something to give the other: she, by asking him to design for her exclusively, had excited and completely satisfied his creative urge; he, by his attentiveness, admiration and never-failing presentability – the perfectly tailored suits, faultless manners, air of sophistication which masked the underlying insecurity they shared – proved to be the companion she had always wanted. For Reginald, with his intense dislike of social life and his tendency to go about Richmond in the same kind of clothes as he wore in the jungle or the Himalayas, had turned out to be the greatest disappointment as a husband.

In the early stages of her marriage – one which she soon realised should never have taken place – Gloria had seriously considered the possibility of suing for a divorce, except that in those days incompatibility was scarcely sufficient grounds. As time wore on, two things held her back: the growing awareness that Reginald's exploits were becoming publicly recognised – for which he could well be knighted – and the fact that even if she could prove the unfaithfulness which she suspected during his prolonged absences, she herself had become a guilty party.

There was often speculation amongst the friends and acquaintances of all three individuals involved, as to whether Gloria and Bertie actually did sleep together; for until they had met it had generally been considered that Bertie, while being superficially attracted to pretty women, had nevertheless had a predilection for members of his own sex. Gradually, such gossip ceased. The two of them were accepted, almost as man and wife. Reginald became more and more a figure in the background, both physically and metaphorically. If he chose to go off and leave his wife for months on end, the situation which had developed was hardly surprising.

After Reginald's death from a severe bout of malaria while still in his late fifties, it had saddened Bertie that Gloria refused to become his wife, especially when the real reason dawned on him. She would no longer have a title. He supposed, regretfully, that he had seen her all along through rose-coloured spectacles, perhaps ones which also gave their wearers tunnel vision. Obsessed with clothing the body he had come to worship, albeit in an aesthetic sense, he had turned a blind eye to her character defects which were many and, he now realised, singularly materialistic.

He watched her becoming more and more imperious, unreasonable and, to his further dismay, putting on weight. The figure he had idolised, bedecked and beautified, began, imperceptibly at first, to spread and sag, despite a succession of cosmetic rejuvenating operations: a lift here, a tuck there. Trying also to turn a blind eye to what she saw in the mirror, Gloria began to drink, which only tended to exacerbate the ravages of advancing years. At times she became vituperative, accusing him of only wanting to marry her for her money.

Increasingly depressed – although, to his credit, he remained remarkably elegant and courteous – Bertie sold his business and took to spending more and more time at his own home, occasionally, in lighter moments, having a room redecorated or giving a small select dinner party, for which he did all the cooking. But most days, he was simply to be seen walking miles along the towpath: a smart, slim, solitary figure nearing the end of his life, with no particular purpose, no family – at least, none which came to visit him – who, in spite of once having played quite a role in fashionable society, had somehow missed out in the general scheme of things.

Now, at the age of seventy-eight, he had just heard he had been left a quarter share in a substantial estate and was suffering from a tumour on the brain.

4

Mildred Treadgold sat on the floor beside an open trunk in the attics of Crane Lodge, a heap of diaries spread out all around her.

She had just chanced upon the last entry which Reginald Rayner had written before he went off on what proved to be his final and fatal expedition: *I dare say the time is soon coming for me to pack it in. If this trip is a success, I may well retire and settle down to editing these scribblings. It would be a change from all those official papers and reports I've been obliged to write over the years. I'll be able to relive some of the more exciting incidents, keep the old memory alive. I'm sure, if Gloria consents, Mildred would help me. She is intelligent, quick and methodical . . .*

Mildred blew her nose. It was becoming cold in the attic. The lovely weather of the previous weeks had suddenly given way to an autumnal snap. She had begun to wonder what she should do about heating when October arrived. It seemed such a wicked waste to switch on the boiler and warm up the whole house just for her sake. She must remember to ask Mr Cory, along with many other things about which she felt she needed guidance, such as the diaries and all the other papers which had come to light, when she had at last managed to find keys which fitted the various locks to the trunks.

It had always surprised Mildred why more investigations had not been done at the time of Reginald's death, although she recollected that many of his effects did not arrive until some months afterwards, having been sent by ship from Alexandria. She had often wondered who, exactly, had seen to their despatch. Gloria had been singularly uninterested, off-hand to the point of rudeness, especially towards the two men who had initially come and prowled round the house for a few days, valuing for probate. They had taken away a lot of papers from Reginald's desk in his study, but they had hardly spent any time in the attics or cellars. Of course, it had been January and Mildred well knew how draughty those places could be at the best of times. The old-fashioned central heating seemed powerless against lack of proper insulation. She recalled how she used to have to implore Joanna not to hang about in those parts of the house during winter for, as a child, she had been chesty and apt to go down with bronchitis far too easily.

Mildred wondered whether, perhaps, being now in the book trade, Joanna might have some helpful suggestions regarding the diaries and, indeed, all Reginald's letters and papers. It seemed such a pity that what appeared to be a delightfully human record of a great man's life should not be brought before the public, especially as it was obviously Reginald's intention for something of this sort to happen. Mildred realised that the task would need a professional hand, someone far more skilled than she herself, however intelligent, quick and methodical Reginald had evidently thought her. She knew that she could only, at best, have been a loyal amanuensis, but *how* she would like to have been just that. She would have done anything for him. After all, she had been in love with him since she was eighteen.

She recalled her very first summer at Crane Lodge, when Bernard was a year old and had already had four different nannies. She had come on the recommendation of a friend of a friend of the Rayner family. She used to wonder in the early stages of her employment just why she had been taken on, for she had no qualifications other than that she was well educated, adored children and was a quiet responsible girl whose father had been badly hit by the 1929 stock market crash. It was therefore imperative that she should earn her own living as soon as possible. Later, with maturity, she came to realise that a trained nannie, young or old, would probably never have lasted long in the Rayner household. For Gloria wanted someone who would do as she was told, was discreet, conscientious and not inquisitive, spoke the King's English and was capable of being left in sole charge while she was out socialising.

Mildred had doted on Bernard and, a few years later, on Joanna. She nursed them, played with them, taught them and altogether took on the role which Gloria, because of her temperament, was unable to fulfil. Yet never once did Mildred make either child feel that their natural – or, rather, in this case, unnatural – mother was falling down on her job. 'Mummy is tired', 'Mummy is resting', 'Mummy has to go out', 'Didn't Mummy look beautiful tonight?' she would say and, for many years, the children accepted such a situation without question.

Mildred did not think that anyone ever suspected how she felt about the children's father except, perhaps, Joanna. Soon after his death, the girl – as she still thought of her – had come to spend a weekend with her mother at Crane Lodge. Over the years Mildred had become ever closer to Joanna, finding in her the compassion which, sadly, her brother lacked. Gloria had been particularly trying that Saturday and, in the evening, Joanna, armed with a sherry decanter and a couple of glasses, had come along to the old nursery quarters – now known somewhat ambiguously as 'Mildred's flat'. Pouring out a drink for each of them, Joanna had said, 'How can you stand it, Mildred? I often wonder why you stayed on after Daddy died.' And Mildred had replied, quite simply, 'I'm sure he would have wished me to.' She remembered Joanna then giving her a long hard look before replying, 'Thank you. God knows where our family would ever have been without you.'

And now, here she was, Mildred thought, entrusted with the clearing up of the family home, prising open locks which were rusted, going through the contents of the strong-room, prying into drawers and cupboards, sorting Gloria's clothes in which her scent, Chanel Number 5, lingered so strongly that Mildred often felt as if her late employer was standing beside her, watching her every movement.

If Reginald had been a hoarder – or, at least, too busy during his spells at home to attend to or sort out his growing collection of memorabilia – Gloria, especially since his death, had been far worse. She regarded her husband's possessions, particularly the 'junk', as she called it, in the attics, as an encumbrance which, so long as it was out of sight, she was determined to put out of mind.

Mildred had occasionally intimated that something

should really be done about Reginald's papers and that she herself would be willing to make a start on them, only to be met by his widow's rejoinder, 'Oh, for heaven's sake, Mildred, why can't you just leave well alone?' Apart from the sale of one or two items of value in the main rooms which Gloria had never liked – an icon, a leopard's head, a few scarabs and ivory ornaments – Crane Lodge remained as it had always been. So long as there was enough investment income going into her bank account, enabling Gloria to maintain herself in the manner to which she was accustomed, that seemed all that mattered. Curiously enough, while ever conscious of her personal appearance, it never appeared to occur to Gloria that this might be enhanced by the beautification of her surroundings. She was not and never had been a homemaker.

As if Mildred did not already know this, it was made all the more apparent to her as she now went about her thankless task. Drawers which she had never hitherto opened, let alone searched, revealed strange assortments of knick-knacks, a mixture of the useless, the tawdry and, possibly, even the precious. Although, thanks to Hugh Cory, the contents of Gloria's five jewel cases had been swiftly deposited at the bank to join the diamond necklace and earrings already there, Mildred was constantly coming across odd brooches, pendants and rings scattered amongst photographs – mostly of Gloria herself – letters and, to the finder's dismay, unpaid bills, sleeping-tablets and empty miniature bottles of spirits. There was a magpie quality about the hoards and, when Mildred came to think about it, Gloria, in old age, bore a certain resemblance to such a bird, with her acquisitive habits and penchant for black and white clothes.

Armed with pencil and clip-board and, as often as not, followed by a restless Jason, Mildred went about making lists, carefully noting down any special queries as and when they came to mind. As the days shortened, so her lists lengthened. Completely unforeseen problems cropped up, such as when Mrs Bradley, from next door, called to enquire about 'Lady Rayner's mink coat which she promised to leave me in her will'. Not long afterwards,

General Fisk telephoned to ascertain the name of the solicitors handling Lady Rayner's estate, as the deceased had given him to understand that the picture of the African chief, which had always hung half-way up the stairs – 'of no great worth, of course, Miss Treadgold, just sentimental value' – would pass to him on Gloria's death. Sentimentality was not an emotion which Mildred would ever have associated with either Gloria or the General.

She did her best not to worry Hugh Cory more than she had to, but she often felt things were getting out of hand. He was unfailingly patient and supportive whenever she did contact him, even offering to come to Crane Lodge personally, if need be. Meanwhile, she kept strict accounts of any domestic expenses, but suggested that as she had been treated so generously in Lady Rayner's will, she did not feel she should be reimbursed for her own services. Hugh Cory had become quite upset about this, saying the work she was doing was beyond price and it might be some time, anyway, before any money could be distributed. When she had actually got around to asking about the heating, he had said that the last thing the Estate wanted – his blanket term for everyone involved – was for her to go down with pneumonia and *of course* she must switch on the boiler now the weather was colder.

Sometimes, as she lay in bed at night, tired but unable to sleep, listening to Jason's snuffling noises in his basket in the corner, Mildred's thoughts turned towards her co-beneficiaries. She had been sorry to learn that poor Mr Fane had had to have quite a serious operation and that, according to a letter from Joanna, Bernard was making difficulties about his late mother's will. It had saddened Mildred that, as he had grown up, he had turned out to be not quite the splendid young man she had hoped he might be. He had been such a dear little boy when she had first known him, a little obstinate and temperamental maybe, but she had made allowances for this because of all the changes of nannies during his very first year. Mildred had hoped that she might have been instrumental in correcting this, that by giving the child stability he would become a less contentious character, yet somehow this was not to be. After he went away to school and she had less influence on him, she became increasingly aware of his defects every time he came home for the holidays.

She still loved him of course. After all, he was Reginald's child, however much she now recognised in him so many of Gloria's traits.

5

Bernard and Felicity were taking George out for the Sunday from his prep school in Hampshire. The boy sat in the back of their BMW listening to them talking. Although they both sounded angry they were not, for once, arguing. It was more as if they were venting their mutual displeasure on George's step-grandmother, who had recently died.

Gloria's death had meant little to the child. He had never really liked going to Crane Lodge unless he could spend most of his time there with Mildred. She kept a splendid collection of children's books in her cupboards, and sometimes she would take him into Richmond Park and tell him quite exciting adventure stories. He often wondered how it was that such a quiet funny old woman knew so much about sleeping in tents and lighting fires at night to keep away wild animals.

Today, he noticed her name kept cropping up in his mother's and stepfather's conversation, along with someone called H and the lady he knew as Aunt Joanna. It seemed to George as if Bernard and Felicity had it in for all of them, especially H and Mildred.

'H,' he heard Bernard say, 'mightn't be too long for this world, but Mildred strikes me as the wiry type who might go on for God knows how many years.'

George was quite shocked that his stepfather appeared to wish them both dead. It seemed so wicked, somehow, even though he himself often felt guilty for hoping something terrible would happen to James Frampton, the worst bully in his form who unfortunately sat next to him.

'It's the selling of the diamond necklace and earrings which gets me,' George next heard his mother expostulating. 'Surely your Freddie Hetherington must see how grossly unfair the will is.'

'Of course he does,' Bernard replied, 'but he doesn't think I've grounds for an appeal. He says it would be impossible to prove that Ma was out of her mind or anything like that, especially with Percy Pemberton one of the executors. And, of course, Joanna obviously wouldn't support me.'

'I always thought your sister was a bit of a nut-case, if you ask me,' Felicity said. 'Does Freddie even advise that you shouldn't consent to a Deed of Variation, as Pemberton suggested, so that you each get a lump sum?'

George began to lose interest. A Porsche had just overtaken them and he hoped Bernard would go in for a bit of a burn-up. He knew his stepfather never liked to be outdone in any way.

To the child's dismay, however, it seemed as if just now Bernard had too many other things on his mind. He and Felicity were still talking about wills and trusts and death when they at last arrived at The Grange for lunch. To make matters worse, the first person George saw as they entered the lounge was James Frampton and his parents. The boys glowered at each other. The grown-ups nodded in an off-hand way. Felicity said she would like a Bloody Mary, George wanted a Coke and Bernard had a double whisky. It turned out to be one of those outings which was definitely not a success. Pouring rain kept them inside for most of the afternoon. George found himself forced to play ping-pong with James, who won three times in a row and then tried to argue points when he at last looked like losing. On the whole, George was relieved when the day came to an end and he was deposited back at school.

On the way home to London that evening, Bernard decided to make a small detour and call in unexpectedly at Crane Lodge. He and Felicity had already made two earlier visits, prowling around and considering what items they might wish to buy in at probate value, however aggrieved they felt that this was the way things might have to be done.

Tonight, they were surprised to find Joanna there, having come to spend the weekend with Mildred. They knew she had a perfect right to do this, but nevertheless they were somewhat disconcerted, Felicity assuming a rather mistrustful manner when it transpired there was no more gin in the drinks cabinet. She listened with ill-disguised impatience when Mildred explained that she did not use Mr Cory's 'float money' to buy alcohol, but that Joanna had kindly brought two bottles of sherry with her.

The atmosphere became even more tense when, after Mildred had tactfully left the three of them alone, Joanna vouchsafed the information that she had taken the opportunity to visit Bertie Fane in the Charing Cross Hospital that afternoon.

'How is the old boy?' Bernard, tired and truculent, stretched out on the sofa, his third whisky of the day – as he had now all but drained the Crane Lodge decanter – on a small table beside him. He had already had the best part of a bottle of wine at lunch.

'Much better than I expected,' replied his sister, brightly. 'They're thinking of discharging him in a week or so.'

'With a nurse, I presume?'

'Maybe initially. Or they might send him to a nursing-home for a while. They're waiting to see how he goes on. Surgeons are so clever, these days. Happily, he could make a complete recovery.'

Bernard, infuriated by Joanna's cheerful optimism, remained silent, as she went on, 'I consulted my solicitor, as Percy seemed to want us all to do with regard to the alternative way of handling the estate, and I've written to let him and Hugh Cory know I'm quite willing to accept income or a lump sum. Apparently Bertie wrote a similar sort of letter before he went into hospital, saying he was prepared to go along with whatever the other beneficiaries thought best. Of course, dear Mildred's done the same. I imagine the ball's in your court now, Bernard, isn't it?'

Suddenly, Felicity broke in, 'Whatever's the point of giving a man who's at death's door, no matter what you think about his health, Joanna, half a million or thereabouts? Besides, it's not as if he has dependants. At least, I don't imagine so.'

'Then in that case,' Joanna replied, levelly, 'you'd prefer to let the will remain as it stands. No Deed of Variation and all of us sharing the income from the trust?'

'Yes, but *what* income?' Bernard became really roused now. 'None of us is going to get all that with the capital being invested by play-safe Percy in long-term gilts.'

'Better than nothing, though,' Joanna persisted. The idea of buying that cottage at Brimley End receded, but she was perfectly philosophical about it. Perhaps, after all, it would be better not to tinker about with Gloria's will in any way. That was how her mother had left it and Joanna had been surprised that Percy Pemberton had even mentioned the other alternative. She hoped sincerely that Bernard had been headed off his idea of actually making an appeal. That *really* would upset everything.

She watched him finish his drink, noticed the heightened colour in his cheeks, wondered once more whether he could be the one to drop dead first, in which case, of course, Felicity, as his wife, would not receive a penny from Gloria's estate. What a hopeless situation they were all in. Momentarily, she felt sorry for her sister-in-law. Felicity must be aware that Bernard was not a good risk but that she, Joanna, was quite a good one. On the other hand, who was to say in what order the four beneficiaries were going to die? Disease and age were not the only things which carried people off. There were accidents, weren't there? Car accidents, for instance. From the look of him, Bernard certainly ought not to be driving back to London. Joanna knew he would feel bound to offer her a lift to Waterloo. Why, they could be killed together and that would leave Mildred and Bertie to share the bonanza, one way or another. She began to feel slightly hysterical, her sudden sympathy for her brother's wife turning quickly to anger on hearing Felicity's next remark.

'I suppose you've been earmarking what you want amongst the goods and chattels?'

'I've noted a few books,' Joanna replied. 'I don't deal in antiquarian ones, as you know, but I thought I'd rather like to buy in one or two of my father's first editions for my own home. And I'm extremely interested in his diaries and letters. I think we should get an expert on to them.'

'I disagree,' Bernard said, loudly. 'I don't fancy the estate paying some clever dick to edit them, if that's what you're thinking of. They might never see the light of day and then where would we be? Money down the drain.'

'Well, I've had a good look at them and I'm pretty sure they're publishable.'

'Look here, Jo.' Bernard suddenly sat up and wagged a finger at her. 'That's only *your* opinion. We don't want to clock up extra expense. Let whoever buys the stuff at auction do the dirty work. That is, if it's saleable. Personally, I can't think who would be interested.'

With alarm, Joanna watched him make a move as if to help himself to the remains of the whisky. Then, to her relief, he was restrained by Felicity saying, 'Better not, Bernard. It's time we were getting back. Taking George out always takes it out of me, as you know. Wet Sundays in a Hampshire hotel are absolute hell as far as I'm concerned.' She stood up and turned to Joanna, 'I suppose you'd like to be dropped at Waterloo, wouldn't you? I've never been able to understand why you don't drive up here.'

Joanna flushed. Felicity had always had an extraordinary capacity for needling her. 'I don't relish long car journeys, especially at night.'

'I don't suppose Bernard and I do, really, but when you have a child at boarding-school, what else can you do? One has to do one's stuff.'

They trooped out of the room. Joanna went upstairs to collect her suitcase and say goodbye to Mildred who followed her down into the hall, where they found Felicity hastily zipping up a small hold-all.

What a miserable trio we are, Joanna thought, as she sat in the back of the car, trying not to look as Bernard swung in and out of the traffic, cursing at the lights and the other drivers, just as he had done when he had driven her back to town on the day of the funeral. Here we all are, very much richer, whichever way the will is finally handled, yet it doesn't seem to have made us any happier. It reminds me of all that trouble I had with Sam Foster when I was getting divorced and he kept urging me to press for a capital sum instead of alimony. I honestly think Mildred and Bertie deserve to come out of all this best. I'm glad I went to see him this afternoon.

Stuck in a traffic jam along the Cromwell Road, Joanna

wondered whether the other two occupants of the car were conscious of the irony as *Money Is the Root of all Evil* came softly over the radio.

6

Bertie Fane sat in the lounge of the Tregarthen Nursing Home, to which he had been sent to recuperate after his operation. It was a luxurious well-run establishment on the south coast, but it did little to alleviate his inherent tendency to depression. He found the atmosphere slightly suffocating, many of the other residents older than himself and their conversation almost totally confined to their ailments, occasionally lightened by references to the weather, the stock market and some younger relatives who might or might not be going to visit them.

Bertie did not expect any visitors. After all, it would be a long way to come, particularly for friends of his own age group. He had been touched when, on separate occasions, Mildred and Mrs Pardoe and Joanna had arrived to see him unexpectedly in the Charing Cross Hospital. Joanna's visit, especially, had been very welcome. He wondered whether, perhaps, when he got home, she might sometimes spend a weekend at Strand-on-the-Green after Crane Lodge had been sold, although he realised how dedicated she was to her little business. It would be nice, he thought, if she married again, but that was evidently not to be. There was this man called Sam, who he believed had let her down in some way. He wasn't sure of the story. Gloria had seemed uninterested.

A gong went for lunch and Bertie got up slowly, steadying himself on the side of his chair and then walking, with the aid of a stick, into the dining-room. He sat by himself at a little table in the corner by a window with a view across the English Channel. It was a grey misty day and the sea was choppy. He wished devoutly he was back home looking out over the Thames.

Bertie knew that, by rights, he ought to be feeling happy and relieved. He had been told that the operation had been a great success. With regular physiotherapy he should be as right as rain, Mr Smithson had said, in six months' time. He wondered why rain was always considered 'right'. It seemed a rather silly sort of metaphor to his way of thinking. The powers-that-be added a warning, of course, that he himself would have to do his bit: regular exercises and adherence to a strict regime. This he fully intended to do. The last thing he wanted was to remain incapacitated, physically or mentally. He had almost finished *The Times* crossword that morning, so he reckoned the old brain-box wasn't doing too badly. He hadn't gone cuckoo as he had feared, but he was certainly far from mobile. He realised it was early days, but unless he was soon able to take more exercise, he knew he might be in danger of putting on weight. He had always prided himself on keeping slim. He felt it was a duty for both men and women to try to do this as they got older. Obesity offended his aesthetic senses.

That morning he had received a letter from Hugh Cory, forwarded by Mrs Pardoe. It would seem that the execution of Gloria's will was going to be far from easy and, reading between the solicitor's carefully worded lines, Bertie had a shrewd suspicion that Bernard was at the bottom of it all. Apparently, Counsel's advice might have to be sought on a number of points, such as a possible Deed of Variation should all the beneficiaries consent to accept a lump sum, the impossibility of any beneficiary successfully appealing against the will in principle and the best method of dealing with the substantial archive which had just come to light. Even a full-scale biography of Reginald Rayner had been mooted.

In his last paragraph, Hugh Cory made reference to the invaluable help of Miss Mildred Treadgold, who had advised that the clearing up of Crane Lodge would take much longer than anticipated, owing to the incredible amount of material which she kept finding.

Poor Mildred, Bertie thought. How he would hate to have been burdened with her job. Muddle of any kind invariably upset him. In his own home his papers were all in immaculate order, anything extraneous having been automatically thrown away. He knew where to lay his hands on whatever was important at any given moment. At least, he reflected, there should be no problems when *he* died. His will was quite clear if, perhaps, surprising.

Bertie ate his lunch slowly, taking care to eschew potatoes, cream and a rather tempting bread roll. It was, he supposed, ridiculous for a *man* – leaving aside all the medical advice he had recently been given – to mind so much about getting fat. Eating and drinking were usually considered one of the few pleasures left to someone of his age. But there it was. A few more pounds on the scales would only add to his depression.

Once back in his room for the obligatory rest that afternoon, he was surprised when there was a knock on the door and a nurse entered with a registered parcel addressed to him. He signed the requested chit and turned it over wonderingly. Postmarked Richmond, he recognised Mildred's writing. On opening it, he read her covering letter which she had stuck with sticky-tape on to a cardboard dress-box. 'Dear Mr Fane,' he read,

When I telephoned Mrs Pardoe to ascertain your correct address, she told me you were getting on well. I am so pleased and do hope you will be able to return home soon.

I thought I should send these letters to you. I feel I could well come across more. I have found most of them in Lady Rayner's bedroom, but others I have discovered in various places about the house, such as behind, as well as inside, certain books in the bookcases. I saw your name at the end, but naturally I have not read any of them.

I am also enclosing these lovely sketches of yours which you made for some of Lady Rayner's outfits etc., together with a bundle of photographs. I trust I am doing right in this, but it all seemed so personal and I would not have thought any of the items belong to the Estate.

If there is anything you would like to earmark to buy in at probate value, please do not hesitate to let me know. Perhaps when you are back at Strand-on-the-Green you would be able to come over here. Judging by the enormity of material still to be sorted, I doubt that Crane Lodge could be sold until well into the New Year.

I should always be more than happy to act as a chauffeur.
With all best wishes,
Yours sincerely,
Mildred Treadgold.

P.S. I remember Lady Rayner going off to the ballet in the tiered tulle dress and thinking it the most beautiful one I had ever seen.

Bertie Fane re-read the letter; he was particularly taken by the postscript. Then he turned to the sketches. They were some of the best he had ever done. They must have been around 1929/1930. His model, based on Gloria, of course, had short bobbed hair, large dark eyes and the slenderest of figures. He could see her now in the dress Mildred had so admired, as well as in the coat with the wide fur collar and fur muff, the little cloche hat he had instructed a colleague to make for her, the pyjama suit with flared trousers, the gold lamé coatee. He closed his eyes. So long ago. Well over fifty years and now, what was at the end of it? Gloria dead; he, at best, an old crock, probably soon for the funeral pyre also. Why was it that youth never thought about dying? Never valued life? Did terrible things, drove too fast, took so many chances? How old was he before he regularly began to study the obituary columns in the papers? Earlier on it had always been the Engagements and Marriages and, of course, those write-ups of parties, luncheons, dinners, all the fun of the fair, as it were, of which he had not been an altogether unknown or unwilling participant, even if he had never been as lighthearted as those with whom he consorted. He had often felt depressed, particularly when he thought of the Depression with a capital D; yet economically it had not really affected him or his ladies. They still wanted dresses. The rich somehow remained rich. Ascot was but a case in point. One couldn't get into the Royal Enclosure if one had been divorced, something of which, he later realised, Gloria was very well aware. But at that time he had simply accepted his role as perfect escort, taking her to watch Helen Wills and Suzanne Lenglen at Wimbledon or to see the first night of Noel Coward's *Cavalcade* at Drury Lane, at which King George V and Queen Mary were present. Gloria's husband might have been half-way up the Amazon, but back home certain other people had better things to do.

Somehow, the photographs which Mildred had sent did not strike nearly such a chord of nostalgia as the sketches which Bertie studied long and hard. Those made Gloria come alive in a way the early snapshots failed to do. Taken with an old Brownie camera which he recalled having bought for ten and sixpence, they were blurred and amateurish. The only really good picture he possessed of Gloria was an oil painting done by an artist friend just before the Second World War. She was wearing an off-the-shoulder black velvet evening dress which Bertie had specially designed for her and the portrait had been considered the best in the 1939 Summer Exhibition at the Royal Academy. This was his most treasured possession which hung in a place of honour above the fireplace in his sitting-room; but as for the photographs Mildred had sent, these meant little to him. He had never enjoyed or mastered the art of photography.

Nor, he realised on picking up the first letter which came to hand, was he much good at letter-writing either. This particular one brought back memories of a different kind, ones on which he preferred not to dwell. It had been written after a terrible row they had had in the summer of 1932. Had he really addressed her so cringingly as 'My Gloria . . .'? He found himself acutely embarrassed at the flowery intimate tone. Why had she kept it, especially as she had always promised to destroy anything he wrote to her? What a fool he had been to believe that she would keep her word. But was she, perhaps, more sentimental than he had given her credit for? Had he meant more to her than he had imagined? There was no order in the letters and he glanced hurriedly through a second one dated January 1937, soon after Edward VIII's abdication. Bertie had been in Paris, but Gloria had been unable to accompany him because Reginald was expected home.

Bertie was amazed at how ardent he himself appeared on paper, far more so than in real life. He felt immensely grateful to Mildred for rescuing such missives and returning them to him. Knowing her integrity, he had absolutely no doubt that she had never read any of them, thank God. Mildred was the soul of honesty and discretion. But how terrible it would have been if others had come across them. Bernard, for instance.

Of one thing Bertie was certain: he would keep the sketches but not the photographs or letters. Indeed, he could not bear to go on reading the latter. They must all be destroyed. But how? He was a sick man, semi-incapacitated. Could he possibly get as far as the pier and drop the box into the sea? That might be best. But he would have to be alone. It wouldn't do to have some nurse watching. And the box was big. He would have to dispose of its contents a little at a time. He began to get fussed. He could feel panic rising within him, just as it did before one of his shows and he knew he would have to walk out into the middle of a roomful of sophisticated ladies and announce the names of his 'creations'. He used to have sleepless nights beforehand. He had never forgotten the time when he had said, 'This is Marianne in *The Sacred Pool*' and how he had distinctly heard old Lady Swanton hissing behind her programme to her neighbour, 'Good God, Bertie's into swimwear now.'

If only he were now at home, everything would have been quite different. He could have torn up the letters slowly, taken his time, and then seen them safely tied up in one of those plastic bags Mrs Pardoe put out for the refuse collectors. But nothing like that could happen at the Tregarthen Nursing Home. The nurses would wonder what he was at. The cleaners would most likely start fishing about in his waste-paper basket. Besides, he wasn't at all sure he was yet up to the physical effort of such a tearing-up operation. He had always used the thickest embossed paper, the kind which he reckoned was helpful because of the snob element in his profession.

Confused, he rang the bell and asked if he might have

tea served in his room: nothing to eat, just a cup as he was feeling a little tired.

He had not bargained on quite such swift solicitude on the part of the authorities. A Sister arrived almost at once and started taking his blood pressure, concerned that he had been overdoing things, although he noticed her eyes stray curiously towards the half opened box. He knew there was not much that got past them at the Tregarthen and her next remark only seemed to confirm this.

'I believe you walked all the way down the drive alone this morning, Mr Fane,' she said. 'I think for just a little longer you should have a nurse to accompany you. You are a model patient, but we don't want any set-backs, do we? You must not be too ambitious at this stage.'

Ambitious or not, Bertie thought, after she had left him, somehow or other he had to get rid of those damn letters all by himself, even if it meant packing them in his suitcase and waiting until he got back to Strand-on-the-Green.

7

Hugh Cory sat in his office in Chancery Lane and asked his secretary, Elaine Tripp, to bring him the Rayner file. In front of him lay a letter he had just received from Mildred Treadgold. She had carefully itemised the points she wished to 'bring to his notice,' as she put it. Mildred was nothing if not correct and efficient.

The first one concerned the damp in the attics at Crane Lodge. 'I felt this should be attended to at once, she wrote, 'so I telephoned Hansons, the local builders, who discovered a loose tile, which they have replaced. While here, however, Mr Peter Hanson remarked that he was not too happy about the possibility of dry rot. I myself have noticed a curious smell when I have been working there. Perhaps you would care to contact them direct about what should be done regarding this?'

Mildred's second point dealt with a certain trunk which she had the greatest difficulty in opening. Here, she had found, beneath a surface covering of old blankets, etcetera, some *artefacts*. This word she had heavily underlined. 'I have no idea how valuable these are,' she wrote, 'but there seem to be one or two ingots, some tribal relics and some coins.' The word *coins* was again underlined. 'I am wondering about insurance,' the letter went on. 'There have been some nasty burglaries round here lately. The Collets, next door, had some silver taken and I thought perhaps this trunk, as well as the others containing all the papers, might be stored in the bank.'

Hugh Cory covered his face with his hands. Gloria's bank was already storing a not inconsiderable amount of jewellery and silver. There was a limit as to what else it could be asked to accept. Besides, trunks took up a great deal of space. He wished he was not feeling so jaded. There had been a law society dinner the previous evening, his wife was unwell and he had promised to try and get home early because she had been complaining that he never saw anything of their children.

He was frankly worried about the Rayner estate and he

45

knew that Percy Pemberton was also. They had been waiting for some weeks now to hear from Bernard. Hugh could not quite make out what the fellow was up to, only that he had switched to another firm of solicitors, from whom, Bernard had once again informed him in the same ominous tone, 'you will be hearing'. Thinking that a letter was on its way, Hugh had decided to hold up applying for probate. It would be helpful to know whether Bernard *was* going to appeal after all or, at least, to know what his feelings were about accepting a lump sum instead of income from a trust.

Wearily, he turned his attention to the Rayner file and then an idea occurred to him. He would take the afternoon off, go by train to Richmond, pay a visit to Crane Lodge and ask Mildred if she would mind driving him back to Kew, where he lived. He knew she still had the use of Gloria's car. He reached for his telephone and asked Elaine to get him through to Miss Treadgold.

Mildred was delighted when she heard what he proposed. Even in the short space of time since she had posted her letter, further problems had arisen. The gardener, who had been off sick, had sent a note by his wife giving in his notice. Mildred had been afraid this might happen, because he had become increasingly surly lately and had hinted that there were one or two other people around needing help, ones who, Mildred suspected, would probably pay much more money. Towards the end of her life, Gloria had adamantly refused to increase his wages, however many times Mildred had pointed out that they were well below the average for the district. She sensed that the man had hung on probably hoping for a legacy and had been extremely put out when this had not been forthcoming and that, all in all, he would now be glad to see the back of Crane Lodge.

Meanwhile, the fallen leaves were mounting up and this was beginning to upset Mildred. She decided she would ask Hugh Cory if she should put an advertisement for a part-time gardener in the local post office. And she would certainly take him up to the attics so that he could smell the dry rot for himself. It had seemed worse than ever that morning, while she had sat there for at least two hours trying to find Reginald's diary for 1949 so that she would have the decade neatly bundled up and be able to start on the 'fifties.

Hugh arrived soon after two thirty, having taken a taxi from Richmond station. He had declined Mildred's offer to collect him from there, saying he was not sure what time he might arrive and did not want her hanging about in such cold wet weather. He made a short inspection of the garden before coming to the front door, stood for a moment looking up at the large forbidding house, shivered slightly and pressed the bell.

On entering, he was distressed to find that Mildred was evidently economising on the central heating. The warmth of her greeting greatly exceeded the chilly atmosphere of the hall. He was relieved when she suggested that he might like to keep his overcoat on until he had toured the attics, where he found the smell she had desscribed certainly most unpleasant. There was, however, plenty of evidence of her diligent work to be seen and he began complimenting her on it. He agreed that the trunks – the archive as he put it – should probably be removed to a safer and less damp environment and promised to try to arrange this within a few days, but for the life of him he couldn't quite think how he was going to go about it. Although he was forty-two, he had never before come up against quite so many peculiar difficulties regarding the execution of a will.

Gradually, he followed Mildred round the rest of the house, saw her neat lists attached by sticky tape to various drawers and chests already sorted, told her by all means to advertise for another gardener, asked how her 'float' money stood, whether she was warm enough, not too nervous after the nearby burglaries and not attempting to do any of the work for which he had given instructions for the cleaning lady to be retained.

To all his solicitous enquiries, Mildred assured him that he had no cause to worry. Her greatest anxiety, she explained, was over the fact that she was not getting on with the clearing-up as fast as she would have liked, to which Hugh Cory replied that owing to certain difficulties his end, there would be no question of selling Crane Lodge .

for quite a little time. For one thing, in order to make any satisfactory sale, the dry rot must be attended to at once. In fact, he asked if he might use the telephone there and then to speak to Mr Hanson.

When he was at last in bed that night, Hugh found himself still unable to push the problems of the Rayner estate out of his mind. He felt infinitely sorry for Mildred, as well as full of admiration. There she was, rattling around alone in a dismal barracks of a place, doing, without complaint, such a depressing laborious job. True, she would eventually be a great deal better off one way or another, but what a wretched life the poor woman must have led. What could it have been like looking after the widowed eccentric Gloria and, to some extent, Reginald, and the children before that? Had Mildred ever thought about herself? Hardly. She was one of life's saints.

A kind of anger began to mount up inside him, anger at the vast discrepancy there was between the goodness and badness – or should he say baseness? – of human beings. What made some so much more avaricious than others and a few, like Mildred, not avaricious at all? The latter were definitely in a minority. Most people, it seemed, wanted more than they had and then, if they got it, wanted more again. Personally, although he did his best not to think about it, he himself could well have done with just a fraction of the estate he was now having to administer. He had a widowed arthritic mother living alone in a small cottage in Kent, about whom he was becoming increasingly concerned, his wife was delicate and he had three young sons to educate. Yet, here he was, trying hard to remain accommodating and perform his duty, particularly in respect of a man for whom he was beginning to have the greatest contempt. For, when all was said and done, Bernard did not look as if he had ever had to deny himself anything, but seemed intent on acquiring far more than his share as a beneficiary under the terms of his late mother's will. Hugh decided if he did not hear from him within the next day or so, he would send a reminder that others were waiting upon his decision.

Hugh did not receive a letter from Bernard the next

morning, but he did hear from Joanna. She said that she had been turning over in her mind the question of her father's papers and she felt that, if skilfully handled, they could be used to make a kind of portrait of him. His diaries and letters would bring such a book to life, she thought, and she then cited a few titles where this method had been adopted with great success. She happened to know someone who would be willing to undertake the task. He was a professional writer and she herself would be prepared to put up the money for him to do this. She went on to say that there was an added reason which had prompted her to make this suggestion. Her friend, Mr Samuel Foster, was a neighbour of hers. They could possibly work together. He would be able to house the trunks and she could provide him with a great deal of background information. Would Mr Cory like to put this to the other beneficiaries? She enclosed a brief list of the said author's works.

On balance, Hugh Cory thought Joanna's idea an excellent and generous one. He was not acquainted with the books Mr Foster had written, but then he was not much of a reader. He had too much of that to do in his chosen profession. But somewhere in the back of his mind, Hugh seemed to recall hearing the name of Foster mentioned on television. The thought of quickly removing such threatened and tricky material from the Crane Lodge attics and having their author's daughter and a friend getting to work on it was certainly an enormous relief. Moreover, it would give him an immediate excuse for writing to Bernard.

What Hugh did not know was that Joanna had already broached the idea when she was speaking to her brother on the telephone and had found Bernard singularly unhelpful. He was slightly mollified by the thought that it would cost him nothing, although he added that he considered she was a damn fool to stump up any money for Sam Foster. He had never quite known why she hadn't married him, only that there had been 'difficulties'. 'It isn't as if you get on all that well with him, is it?' he asked, to which Joanna had replied that whatever misunderstanding there had been between them in the past, it would make no difference to their working together now.

49

After she had rung off, Joanna hoped she was right in saying this. Her relationship with Sam had been rather an unusual one and, at times, stormy. After her marriage to a charming but totally feckless young man had inevitably broken up, she thought she had found in Sam a shoulder to lean on, as well as a kindred spirit. For one thing, he was considerably older than she was and, at the time, a minor literary figure. He had written for both radio and television, was the author of several well-received travel books, a regular contributor to the local journal in the area in which she had opened her bookshop and was currently embarking on a novel. Joanna found him attractive, mentally and physically. His quick mind and lighthearted bantering and obvious admiration helped her enormously while she was still in the process of getting a divorce – that is, when they first became acquainted.

Then, several things began to bother her. One was that Sam wanted to sleep with her and she with him. Yet the new divorce laws had not quite come into force and she was acutely aware that she was suing Francis, her husband, for adultery. She had obtained a Decree Nisi but the Absolute had been held up because her almost ex-husband was being difficult about a settlement. The fact that she had been helped financially by her father made Francis less inclined to pay up. She was having to cope with lawyers, the shop and Sam who, thwarted by her refusal to go to bed with him, was now talking about matrimony. She did not want to lose him, but she was uneasy when he kept urging her to try to get a lump sum out of 'that mean bastard', as he kept calling Francis, instead of alimony. When she pointed out that she had been subsidised by her father and could not understand why Sam was so insistent, he said, 'Don't be a fool, Jo. You may have worked in bookshops earlier on, but you've taken a hell of a gamble now and you must realise that alimony stops on remarriage.'

Bewildered and saddened, she refused to see him for quite some time. But one evening he came into the shop just as it was closing. She was feeling particularly depressed. The business was not doing well. Sales were down and she was afraid Sam might have been right in his fears about her solvency. Then, quite suddenly, from the pocket of his duffel coat, he produced a bottle of champagne, which he proceeded to open in her little back office. He spent that night with her in her flat above the shop.

Joanna was still not quite divorced and she felt immensely guilty about what had taken place. Her lawyers had been frankly puzzled for some time about her indifference to what they called her 'rightful claims'. Now, she took them completely by surprise by saying that she had decided to abandon any claims whatsoever. In the event, they obtained a small amount of alimony, her Decree Absolute was granted and she and Sam went off for a long weekend together. To his credit, he did not upbraid her. The subject was never mentioned again. Both realised that matrimony was out and that the situation between them was probably better as it was. They maintained separate establishments, he in a converted stable block of a large country house in the district, she in her flat above the shop.

Gradually, their individual circumstances improved. Sam's books, though never best-sellers, began to procure for him a wider public, if not an equivalently larger income. Joanna, after many teething troubles, found the shop bringing her in a reasonable income. When she had told Bernard on the evening of her mother's funeral that it meant everything to her, she had not been far from speaking the truth. That Sam Foster was still in the background of her life was, perhaps, an added bonus, but one she preferred to keep to herself.

8

It was going to be a curious Christmas to say the least, Mildred thought, as she drove into Richmond to do some last minute shopping. It had all come about because she had declined her brother's invitation to go up to Darlington to spend it with him and his family. Arnold had been quite upset about this. 'It isn't as if you're tied to the old lady any more,' he had said on the telephone. 'You're a free agent.'

But that was what Mildred felt she very definitely was not. She might not have the eccentric demanding Gloria to look after, but she did have Crane Lodge; and as the weeks passed, the place seemed increasingly to consume all her energies. Sometimes it was almost as if it were like an all-devouring monster, constantly lurking, pitting its wits against hers, refusing to give up its secrets or taking a perverse delight in suddenly presenting her with the unexpected. She had, when all was said and done, become accustomed to her former employer's strange whims and fancies. Trying as they were, they were an on-going thing which she had come to accept.

With Crane Lodge, however, it was different. After a long day she often felt it was testing her out, mocking her, as it threw up yet another of Bertie's letters or caused her to twist an ankle – fortunately only mildly – as a floorboard gave way in the furthermost corner of the attics. That was the time she had gone to investigate an old knapsack which, on up-ending, had yielded nothing but a crumpled faded photograph of she knew not whom but which, because of the pain in her foot, she had taken down to her own quarters to study at a later date.

She realised that Arnold, a good brother if somewhat authoritative, only had her best interests at heart when he kept urging her to have a break, saying, 'It would do you good, Milly, to get away.' And often, in the weeks leading up to Christmas, she felt how nice it would be to have a respite from having to heave and lug and sit on the floor confronted by a mass of unaccountable objects and papers.

Yet, all the same, she knew she couldn't have accepted his invitation, however much she would have liked to have seen him and his wife, Rosie, and their children and grandchildren. It probably wouldn't have been the most peaceful of Christmases, but it would have been different, and Mildred would have welcomed a chance to make contact with the younger generation again, whom one day she hoped would benefit from her own estate.

For although Mildred was quite relieved to have just heard that there was now going to be no alteration whatsoever to Gloria's will – Bernard, for reasons best known to himself and his new solicitors, having apparently vetoed even a Deed of Variation whereby each beneficiary would receive an equal capital sum – she was astute enough to realise that her own circumstances might soon be such that her increased income would greatly exceed her modest wants.

So she had abided by the dictates of her conscience and stuck to her post. None of Arnold's cajoling could quite erase from her mind the fact that some time in the coming year Crane Lodge would have to be sold; and for the sake of all involved, it was up to her to see that this could come about smoothly and swiftly whenever it was so desired. Moreover, there was another major aspect to her responsibilities. There was still a spate of break-ins being reported in the local press. Richmond Park seemed a veritable haunt of burglars waiting to nip over the fence into the grounds of the large houses which backed on to it. The workmen who had come to deal with the dry rot had been forced to erect scaffolding. The job was by no means finished and Mildred wanted to make quite sure they not only removed their ladders on Christmas Eve, but took them right away with them. She was not a nervous type, but the place could be extremely vulnerable at this time of the year if it were obviously uninhabited. Indeed, even her temporary absence would prove another headache for Hugh Cory *vis à vis* the insurance company. And there was always Jason to consider. She did not think her brother and his wife altogether took to dogs.

Therefore having finally given in to his sister's steadfastness of purpose, Arnold had suggested that if she definitely refused to come north for the festive season, then she should have a friend to stay with her. This had set Mildred thinking. Why not ask Joanna if she would like to spend what Mildred felt sure, whatever happened, would be the last Christmas in her old home. She might like to bring that man who was going to write something about Reginald. And while she was about it, Mildred thought it would be only kind to invite Bertie Fane over for the day, now that he was back home at Strand-on-the-Green.

Pleased with her idea, Mildred even wondered whether Bernard and Felicity might care to drop in for a drink and it would have been nice to extend some hospitality to Hugh Cory and his family, although she realised that this really would be going a bit too far. A hard-pressed solicitor would scarcely want to mix work and pleasure at Christmastime.

Nevertheless, the warmth of the responses she received from both Joanna and Bertie were most encouraging. Joanna said she would love to come and rang back within half an hour to say that Sam Foster would very much like to accompany her. Apart from all else, he felt it would help him considerably with the portrait of Reginald he was working on and he would welcome an opportunity of talking to Mildred about him. For an agonising moment she wondered whether he and Joanna would expect to share a bedroom, but then she put such a thought right out of her mind. So far as she knew, they were simply friends with a common interest in literature. Besides, Joanna was a lady. Whatever her private life, she would always behave impeccably in public, especially on a Christmas visit to her late mother's home. Mildred found she had gone quite pink, angry with herself for ever having entertained the idea. It had been a relief to get quickly on the telephone and speak to Bertie.

He said nothing would give him greater pleasure than to come to Crane Lodge for Christmas lunch and that he was most grateful for her offer of transport, although he would be more than happy to hire a car. He also mentioned that he was sure Mildred would understand if he 'faded out', as he put it, after the Queen's speech in the afternoon, as it would be his first social outing since his illness, but one to which he would look forward immensely.

After this, Mildred felt almost in duty bound to ring up Bernard. Crane Lodge, after all, had been his family home as well as his sister's. She could not very well ask Joanna and not invite her brother and his wife to join in some part of the festivities, although she trusted if they did drive over their visit would be a short one.

Mildred had never felt quite easy whenever Bernard and Felicity had been in the house lately, especially since the time she had come downstairs with Joanna to say goodbye to them and found Felicity hastily zipping up a small hold-all. Mildred had already been aware that Bernard's wife had a habit of nosing round in chests and cupboards containing items still to be sorted. Mildred had done her best not to think the worst, for if Felicity *had* found some trinket or other which she had appropriated, there was nothing much anyone could do about it, and it would therefore be best to give the woman the benefit of the doubt. It had been a nasty shock after that particular day when Mildred had discovered that Reginald's carriage clock – which she happened to know was quite valuable but had lain for a long time in need of repair in the top drawer of his desk – was no longer there. For this reason alone, she felt that Felicity would hardly want to spend much time at Crane Lodge while Bertie and Joanna and her friend were there.

To her surprise and consternation, however, Mildred found she was wrong. On broaching the subject to Felicity – for unfortunately it had been she who had answered the telephone – Mildred at first thought that her eagerness actually to come to Christmas lunch was because she was afraid that the other beneficiaries might be going to steal a march on her in some way. Then Mildred realised it had much more to do with the fact that Felicity was going through one of her not infrequent periods of domestic problems. Her Filipino maid had apparently departed at short notice and she was having trouble finding a re-placement. She herself was not feeling at all well and

George was bringing a small friend, called Tim, to stay for
the holidays as his parents were abroad. (She omitted to
say that in ordinary circumstances she always found it
easier to cope with two children rather than one, as it
absolved her from the responsibility of having to keep her
own child amused.)

What Felicity *did* say, however, was that she and Bernard
had been thinking of lunching at a Mayfair hotel on Christmas Day, which was not exactly an ideal solution for
children. A roast turkey at Crane Lodge would be so much
better. Bernard's wife became quite expansive at this point,
adding that Mildred's invitation was really heaven-sent.

Mildred had certainly not bargained on giving Felicity
and Bernard lunch and, much as she loved children, she
somehow hadn't reckoned on George coming into the
picture, let alone his friend. When faced with this new
development, she started counting up and realised that
she would have to cater for double the number anticipated.
She even began thinking it might have been better to have
gone to Darlington after all and let Hugh Cory bother
about the security of the house. But, being a woman who
invariably stuck to her principles, she simply sat down at
the kitchen table, made longer lists, increased her orders
and hoped for the best.

Two days before Christmas, therefore, found her off to
collect a fourteen-pound turkey, a variety of fresh vege-
tables, various other delicacies, three bottles of quite a
good claret – about which she had been careful to take the
advice of the manager of the wine shop – and a small
Christmas tree. It never occurred to her that those partici-
pating in the occasion might contribute towards it materi-
ally which, in the event, Bertie and Joanna insisted on
doing. All her life, Mildred had been the one who gave and
now, with her windfall in the offing, it seemed perfectly
natural that the onus of Christmas should be on her.

Methodically, she ticked items off her list as she pur-
chased them, decided that a large jig-saw might keep her
guests happily occupied, even if intermittently – she had
already bought them all individual presents, including
the children – and then, quite by chance, as she was

walking back to the car, she saw in a shop window a dress which took her fancy. It was a grey woollen affair with a high collar, a white bow at the throat and a pleated skirt.

It was so long since Mildred had bought any new clothing for herself, yet the more she looked at the dress the more she felt it would suit her. And, after all, she reasoned, why ever not? She had already spent far more than she had anticipated on Christmas, but there was money coming her way, wasn't there? Hitherto, she had always abided by her mother's maxim, instilled into her in youth: *though one's wants may be many, one's needs are few.* Strictly speaking, of course, she didn't *need* a new dress. The one she had worn each Christmas Day for nine years would do perfectly well. But somehow she couldn't help *wanting* what was in the window. Surely it would be a justifiable extravagance?

With an almost jaunty step, Mildred entered the dress shop.

9

'A most delicious meal. I think we should all drink a toast to the cook,' said Bertie Fane, raising his glass and looking at Mildred. There was a chorus of enthusiastic 'Hear, hears!' except for Bernard, who finally muttered a somewhat grudging, 'Er, yes, excellent.'

Mildred, in her new dress, unusually flushed and looking surprisingly rather pretty, replied, with customary modesty, 'Thank you, but I could never have managed without Joanna. She did all the donkey work,' to which the latter answered, again with suitable self-deprecation, 'I don't call peeling spuds much of a hardship. In fact, it's rather a soothing occupation. And I only came in at the last minute, so to speak. It's all the organisation beforehand that counts. Mildred was always so good at that. I've never forgotten the trouble she went to over filling Bernard's and my stockings when we were small.'

Bernard glowered at his sister. He did not want to be reminded of when he was small and, with his heavy features and red-veined nose, it was difficult to imagine that he ever had been.

Thinking of children, Mildred turned to George. 'Would you and Tim like to go up to my flat now? I don't expect either of you want coffee. You could take your presents with you' – she had bought them each a game – 'and you'll find quite a few books up there which you might care to look at.'

The boys disappeared with alacrity but, once in the old nursery quarters, Tim said he would like to explore the rest of the house. George, who was not an adventurous child except in his desire to be driven fast in cars, was much more inclined to open up the games which Mildred had given them but being, as it were, host, he felt obliged to show his friend round Crane Lodge. When they came to the foot of the stairs leading to the attics, he remarked, 'I don't think there's much to see up there.'

'But it's where the dry rot is, i'n't it? Wot the old girl was on about at lunchtime?' Tim was possessed of many qualities which George seemed to lack. He had spirit, initiative and an enquiring mind, although he had a shocking accent which both Felicity and Bernard privately deplored.

'Yes, I suppose so.'

'Well then. We could go and 'ave a look. I've never seen dry rot.' Tim had already started to mount the stairs. George, unwillingly, followed. He had never had occasion to visit the attics before. There seemed something sinister about the place. He had no idea what dry rot looked like and cared less.

'I'n't there a light?' Tim was by now standing in the first attic, his round cherubic face appearing a sickly shade of green in the all-pervading gloom.

George looked about rather hopelessly, until Tim suddenly said, 'There 'tis. Behind you.' George stepped back obediently and pressed the switch. Once illuminated, the room revealed nothing but a neat row of trunks with labels and lists attached to them.

'What did I tell you?' he said, shivering a little. 'There's nothing much up here.'

'Not in this attic, maybe, but there's more to see further through.'

'I don't want to go further through. Let's go back downstairs and play those games we've been given. The detective one looks quite good.'

'We could play real 'tecs up here. We could pretend there's a body. C'mon.' Tim marched straight into the second attic, found another light switch and whistled, appreciatively. 'This is more like it. Look, see that little trap door over there in the wall? I bet there's a secret or two behind that.' He went purposefully across and began tugging at the bolts which appeared to be securing a metal panel.

'I don't think you should do that. I don't think Mildred would like it.' George was feeling distinctly uneasy.

'I'm only *looking*. I expect it's where the dry rot is. We could probably get out on to the roof this way. And no one's to know. Old Mildew's too busy entertaining your Mum and all the others downstairs.'

Tim removed the trap door and a blast of icy air blew straight into their faces. He then dragged a tin box towards the aperture, raised himself up on it and peered through. He let out a whoop of triumph. 'There, wot did I tell you? It leads out on to the roof. I can see a bit of the garden below.'

'Come back!' George was by now thoroughly scared. He knew what his stepfather was like when angry and that this was always worse when he had had anything to drink. He had observed that Bernard had been by far the most heavy imbiber at lunch. He and Sam Foster had done more than full justice to Mildred's claret. Felicity had had one or two fill-ups but Bertie Fane and the other ladies had hardly drunk anything in comparison. If Bernard were to come up to the attics now, there would be all hell to pay. 'Come back, Tim,' he repeated, but his friend paid no notice.

In what seemed only a matter of seconds, Tim had wriggled through the aperture and dropped down on to the other side, leaving George to take his place on the tin box but without making any attempt to follow suit.

'Strewth!' Tim, pleased with himself, appeared to be in some kind of gutter, the sloping side of the tiled roof on one side of him, a low stone parapet, no more than two feet high, on the other. The sheer drop down to the garden below made George feel sick.

After a while, it seemed that possibly Tim himself was having second thoughts about his exploit. At the other end of the gutter lay a similar trap door to the one he had come through, but this was obviously firmly secured from the inside. The roof on his right was at too much of a gradient to climb. There was nothing for him to do and nowhere for him to go other than to return the way he had come.

But this presented an unexpected problem. Tim was short for his age. It had been quite a drop down on to the parapet. He had no tin box to stand on and, indeed, nothing on which to gain a foothold at all. Quite suddenly, his bravado deserted him. He began to cry, loudly.

George, still feeling sick and deathly frightened, as much for himself as for his friend, began to join in.

'Get help,' roared Tim, in between bawls. 'I can't get back. Go and get help.'

Still sobbing, George stumbled back through the attics, down the stairs past Mildred's flat and down again to the main hall, where he burst into the drawing-room, just as the Queen was saying, 'God bless you all.'

It was Mildred who reacted most swiftly. A lifetime's experience of children and what they might get up to – although even she could hardly have envisaged what had just taken place – sent her running up the stairs at the mention of George's one word, 'Attic'. Joanna and Sam were quick to follow her, with Felicity and a lumbering Bernard bringing up the rear. Only Bertie Fane, obviously concerned but still finding stairs a slight problem, remained in the hall, looking upwards.

It was Sam Foster who saved the day or, rather, the child. He was a strong man, still thin and agile enough to squeeze through the trap door and let himself down beside a now snivelling Tim. He then lifted the boy into the arms of a furious Bernard who, once the drama was over, gave vent to a string of blasphemous epithets which even Felicity had never before heard him use, at least not in public.

The party broke up quickly after that. Bernard hustled his wife and the boys into their car. Joanna drove Bertie back to Strand-on-the-Green. It was left to Sam Foster to assist Mildred – vigorously doing her best to dissuade him – with clearing up lunch. There had never been a dishwasher at Crane Lodge because, by the time such an innovation had come in to everyday use, Gloria had entertained so little that there had hardly been any need for it. But today, Mildred would have welcomed one. Tim's escapade had upset her more than she liked to admit and her hands shook a little, as she stacked the dirty plates and plunged the silverware into the sink to soak. The day to which she had looked forward, into which she had put so much thought and hard work and which, despite her fears, had augured unexpectedly well in the beginning, had all but ended in disaster.

Sensing her distress, Sam said, 'How about you and me

sitting down and having a quiet cup of tea together? Joanna and I can see to all this later. It's time you had a rest.'

She looked at him gratefully. It really would be rather nice, she felt, to shut the kitchen door, at any rate for just a little while, on all the clutter. 'Thank you,' she answered. 'If you wouldn't mind making up the drawing-room fire, I'll put the kettle on. And I believe there are a few questions you want to ask me about Sir Reginald, aren't there?'

'More than a few,' he replied, smiling. 'After all, you knew him longer than Joanna.'

'Oh, yes.' The flush which had made her seem quite animated at lunch had faded by now although, momentarily, it threatened to return. He thought Joanna had probably been right in surmising that Mildred had been in love with her employer since the day she first stepped inside Crane Lodge.

When she brought the tea and came to sit opposite him by the fire, she suddenly seemed old and tired. He hoped it would not tax her too much to talk about Reginald. Sam Foster was not an altogether bad man, nor an insensitive one. As a struggling author, he might have once been a little too keen on the material aspect of things, but he had his points. He recognised the woman before him as being a cut above the rest of humanity. Even her name intrigued him. Treadgold.

Very gently, he began his interrogation.

10

'Will you be all right?' Joanna was loath to leave Bertie by himself, especially on Christmas evening.

'Oh, yes. You don't need to worry. Mrs Pardoe, bless her heart, is coming back at seven. She's been sleeping here regularly since I returned from the nursing-home and refused to make any alterations over the holiday, except to go to her married son's for the day when she knew I'd been invited to Crane Lodge.'

'I'm glad. She'll carry on like this, will she?' Joanna was still perturbed. He seemed so frail, so old and so alone. But Bertie, for all his somewhat troubled life, was not a leaner.

'Yes. She pops back to her own house during each day. Being a widow now, I think, for two pins, she'd like to move in here permanently, but . . . well, her own home's her security, isn't it? I wouldn't want her to give it up and, really, I've become so used to my own company.'

It crossed Joanna's mind that Mildred might eventually join up with Bertie, but then she dismissed the idea. Surely Mildred had had enough of looking after others. It was high time she had a rest and a little place of her own. Joanna wondered how she and Sam Foster were making out together. It was six o'clock and they would probably be expecting her. For all she knew, perhaps Bertie would welcome an hour or so to himself.

She was on the point of standing up when he said, 'How's the book on Reginald coming along? Sam didn't seem to want to say too much about it at lunch.'

'Slowly,' she replied. 'He's very thorough. And he never likes talking too much about what he's doing. There's an awful lot of reading to be got through and he keeps finding extra material amongst the diaries, letters and things.'

'Letters?' Bertie's head went up. 'What sort of letters?' She thought he looked scared.

'Oh, mostly official, like the ones in the other trunks. You know, from quite well-known people. Some in the Government of the day. They're fascinating. But Sam thinks we might have to take out insurance against libel if he wants to quote from them. One never knows. There might be some old chap . . .' She hesitated, wishing she had not used the expression. 'Or, at any rate, his heirs,' she went on, hurriedly, 'who might sue, although I don't think you can sue a dead person. But there's some pretty pertinent passages in a few I've read. Most of them concerning the conduct of the war. Hugh Cory's going to take Counsel's advice about it. I never knew before that although a letter might belong *physically*, as it were, to the recipient, the copyright belongs to the sender. It's all madly complicated. I can't believe there can be many estates which have such problems. I suppose more should have been done at the time of Reginald's death, only my mother wouldn't allow it.'

Bertie seemed to take so long in replying that she wondered if, perhaps, she had offended him in some way or whether he was just tired. This time she stood up, purposefully, as he said, 'Yes, it's a mistake to hang on to things although, of course, historians and biographers wouldn't say that. From the point of view of the book you and Sam are working on, I expect the diaries and letters are invaluable.'

'Yes. But one mustn't forget it's only a *portrait*, not a biography. So much of Reginald's personal life . . .' She broke off, flustered.

'All individuals,' he replied, slowly, doing his best to put her at her ease, 'are entitled to a certain amount of privacy. I don't expect Sam is in any way overstepping the mark, is he?'

'Oh, no. I think the end result will be very good.'

After he had wished her goodbye and heard her let herself out, he sat back in his chair, staring out of the window across the Thames, thinking of all she had told him, recalling her sudden embarrassment, wishing that he had got to know her better. He thanked God Mildred had seen fit to send him back all his own letters which she had found, even to a small packet pressed into his hand that very day as he was departing. He hadn't been able to get rid of the main collection at the Tregarthen, but he had made quite sure he saw them into the refuse van as soon as he got home, along with any letters from Gloria which he had kept. Strictly speaking, according to Joanna's information, he supposed that the ones he had written to her mother belonged to her estate, but he wasn't going to let that worry him. He'd been a fool to write them in the first place, even more of a fool to believe she had torn them up on receipt. It had taken him a long time to learn that what Gloria said and what she did were two entirely different matters.

He made a mental note that, health permitting, he would once again go through all his own memorabilia in the coming months. He knew just where everything was, he had already been fairly ruthless, but there was always scope for extra culling. There must be nothing for prying eyes to come across. He began to wonder who, exactly, would be responsible for clearing up after him at Strand-on-the-Green. His solicitors, presumably, unless he decided to divulge a secret. He could do so now, really. There was nothing to stop him, save for a promise made a long time ago and, of course, the fear of how much it might hurt.

He felt in his pocket for the packet of letters Mildred had just given him. Once again, he had a great disinclination to read them, but curiosity made him glance at the one on the top, dated December 1943. It was purely formal, explaining to Gloria the difficulty of producing a certain garment for her. They did not see or communicate with each other nearly so much during the war years. For one thing, Reginald was mostly at home, working in Whitehall. Because of his knowledge of places such as the Far East, particularly Malaya, he was invaluable to the Intelligence Service. For another, clothes rationing curtailed much of Gloria's hitherto reckless extravagances in the world of fashion; although Bertie had never ceased to marvel at the ingenuity, determination and often downright dishonest practices which made some women still regularly able to renew their wardrobes at that time. It was nothing to be brought a suit belonging to a husband – often Reginald – and to be asked to cut it up and refashion it. Then, of course, there were always women in another class of society – how he had come to hate the word 'class' – who were willing to sell their clothing coupons to others, such as Gloria, who were always more than willing to pay for them.

He remembered well how the latter managed to get their uniforms made by some designer or other. He himself had seen to it that Gloria looked absolutely stunning in a figure-hugging outfit to wear for her somewhat spasmodic work in the Women's Voluntary Service. He felt uncomfortable now when he thought about it. Advancing years had produced in him a rejection of many of his former values. Retirement and living alone had given him plenty of time for reflection, for self-analysis. His priorities had changed. He had read something somewhere about solitary trees growing stronger. He supposed that perhaps mentally he had done that, although certainly not physically. He wondered what would have happened if he had been more of an age and possessed a better physique so that he could have fought in the last war, instead of spending his days clothing women like Gloria and many a night fire-watching on the roof of his fashion house. It was, he knew, pointless to speculate, to have recriminations. It was more than likely he would now be dead. Instead, he was an old man, a sick one. His life was over, or as good as.

All the same, he kept thinking about the past, the present and what might have been. Shakily, he got up and helped himself to a weak whisky and soda, before settling back in his chair. Felix jumped up on to his lap and he stroked him, absently. Presently, he switched off the lamp by his side and sat in the darkness, watching those other lights across the water. The letter he had just read made him keep thinking about the war, the darkened room reminded him of the black-out. He thought of the first time the Luftwaffe had attacked London. September 7th, 1940. A Saturday it was. He remembered it quite clearly, how there had been two sunsets: a natural one to the west and a man-made one to the east, where there was a glow in the sky as if the whole of that end of London was on fire. He had been playing tennis, of all things, with some friends in Hampstead.

He became so wrapped up in his thoughts that he failed to hear Mrs Pardoe letting herself into the house and was startled when another light was snapped on and he looked up to find her standing at the doorway, saying, 'All alone then, Mr Fane? I hope you had a good day.'

'Oh, yes. Yes, thank you. And you?' His manners and courtesy towards others, especially those he employed, were always faultless. Everyone in his fashion house – models and seamstresses alike – had loved him.

'Mustn't grumble. Bit tired, though. It's my grand-children that get me down. 'Course it's the parents' fault. Spoilt, that's what they are. All them toys.'

He wondered whether he should tell her about Tim's escapade, but decided against it. He did not want to enter into any longer conversation now. He was weary and Mrs Pardoe had admitted that she was, too.

He merely smiled and gave a little nod. Then he said, 'I've always thought Christmas hard on the older gene-ration. I think perhaps I'll have an early night. After Miss Treadgold's excellent lunch, please don't bother to get me anything else to eat. Felix seems to be the one who is feeling hungry.' The cat had already jumped down from his lap and was winding himself round Mrs Pardoe's feet.

'But you must 'ave a little soup, sir. Keep body and soul together.'

Seeing that she looked perturbed, he agreed, but the idea of keeping body and soul together at his age struck him as slightly macabre. While Mrs Pardoe had gone into the kitchen, he sat on, quite still, waiting and wondering. This time of year the thought of the next one always increased his depression. Would he see another Christmas? He doubted it; but he did not mind. He would like just a little longer, perhaps, to go through his things; but he was really ready to go. It was the fear of becoming completely immobile, totally dependent on others, ending up permanently in some Home for Incurables, which haunted him. He supposed, of course, there was always one solution. He could end things himself. He had always been interested in euthanasia and suicide had often crossed his mind. But he knew, when it came to the point, he would never have the courage. He could only wait, just as he was waiting now, for Mrs Pardoe to bring his soup.

Tomorrow, he thought, he would make a big effort to take a longer walk. He might even be able to throw those letters he had just received into the Thames by himself, rather than wait for those refuse collectors – as they liked to call themselves – to arrive. God knew when that would be. Christmas seemed to go on and on these days.

11

'How much do you mind, Jo, about the personal side of your father's life coming out in this book? I mean, the marriage and all that. You've never said much about it.'

It was an unusually mild day in February. Joanna and Sam were walking along an old ox drove where on either side of them the downs rolled away, delicate shades of green and blue mingling in the early spring sunlight.

She took quite a time to reply. Then she said, quietly, 'I suppose I've never said much, because there's never been much to say. I was never close to either of my parents. Mildred is the one I remember most from my childhood. My mother seemed always out, Reginald away, Bernard at boarding-school and Bertie very much in the background.'

He noticed how she almost always referred to her father by his Christian name, as if he were some kind of vague adjunct to the household, a guest who came and went.

'But there must have been times when you and your parents were together. Did they seem unhappy?'

'Oh, no. I don't think they were. There were never any rows, at least not that I was aware of. It was all very civilised. Perhaps they did things better in those days.'

For a while they walked on in silence. Presently Sam said, 'Do you think Reginald was born with a wanderlust?'

'Or did it start through wanting to get away from Gloria?' She finished the query for him.

'You said it. Not I. But one can't help wondering. It seems to have been such a strange marriage from the beginning.'

'Well, don't forget that Reginald had money and was what you might call well-connected. His own father was knighted for political services. I think my mother's parents pushed the match. And, of course, Gloria was very beautiful and saw it as an entrée into the social life she craved.'

'Except that she must have pretty soon become disillusioned. From all you've told me and from what I've read, he absolutely hated that kind of thing.'

'Yes. That's where Bertie came in, even though it was initially she who took him around, as it were.'

'Anyway, to get back to what I was saying. Something of this sort will have to figure in the book. You know, human interest. Reginald seems to shy away from that, but it can't be merely a catalogue of his achievements, although I admit that some of those entries make marvellous reading by themselves.'

'You're not thinking of changing course, are you? Just editing them or, alternatively, going in for a full-scale biography?'

'No. I'd far rather stick to the portrait idea. But it isn't as straightforward as I'd once hoped. I want to make quite sure how you feel about the portrayal of a few characteristics and idiosyncrasies. And I'll need to have a word with Bernard and, maybe, Bertie. After that awful débâcle on Christmas afternoon, there hasn't been a chance.'

'As far as Bernard is concerned, I think he probably just hopes the book will make money for the estate as a whole.'

'What made him change his mind about appealing against the will or even accepting a quarter share-out?'

'I'm not sure.' Joanna had a theory but she preferred to keep it to herself.

'And Bertie? What do you think he thinks about what I'm trying to do?'

Once again, she side-stepped the issue. 'It's difficult to know. He's so pathetic somehow.'

'Well, maybe he'll die before the book gets published.'

'*Sam!*' All the old resentments against him came pouring back. He was such a strange mixture of nice and nasty, Joanna thought. She began to wish she had never proposed him for the job of authorship. But it was too late to back out now. An agent had expressed approval after reading a synopsis and one or two of the more vivid entries in the diaries. There was a hint of trying to obtain quite a substantial advance against royalties, in which Sam was to have a share. Meanwhile, Joanna was subsidising the project in the hopes that, now probate had at last been obtained, it would not be all that long before a trust could be set up and they could each expect some kind of income. It was, perhaps, an odd arrangement, but then everything about the present situation seemed odd.

Sensing that he had upset her, Sam quickly changed the subject. 'How about asking your brother and his wife down here for lunch next Sunday? It's a pity we can't all be friends over this. And, after all, it's not you Bernard's so against. It's the others being treated equally.'

'We could do, I suppose. I'll give them a ring this evening. Bernard's never actually seen where I live. I think he finds a sister like me, living over her shop, beyond his comprehension, as well as pretty demeaning.'

When, however, Joanna extended her invitation to Felicity on the telephone, she was informed, curtly, that it would be impossible to accept as Bernard was away from home. After some further brief guarded remarks, Felicity said, 'Well, you might as well know. Your precious brother's being dried out.'

'*Dried out?*' Joanna was perfectly acquainted with the expression which, for all its serious implications, had always struck her as somewhat comic. It gave her visions of alcoholics stretched out prone under artificial heat, their saturated torsos visibly shrinking to their normal size.

'Don't sound so shocked.' Felicity seemed to be switching her resentment on to Joanna. 'You must have been aware that Bernard's been drinking far too much for a long time. He lost his driving licence coming back from Crane Lodge at Christmas, not that he was anywhere near as over the top as he usually is. Anyway, the upshot of it all is that he's gone to one of those health places which specialise in his kind of problem. God knows if the treatment will do any good. I'm not all that optimistic.'

'How long will he be there?'

'Another fortnight, if he sticks it out. I don't know if he'd feel like coming down to you after that. It would mean my driving and you know how tiring I find being at the wheel for any length of time. It's bad enough having to go alone to visit George at school. Besides, I don't think Bernard wants to be reminded of the estate again. Gloria's will upset him so much. That's what made his trouble

71

worse. He used to get so angry about it and a double whisky every time he received a lawyer's letter, especially one advising him that it would be better not to tinker about with the will in any way, wasn't exactly helpful, was it?'

'No.' Joanna was appalled. She'd known, of course, that her brother drank too much, but she supposed that she had been singularly obtuse in not realising the problem was so serious. Now, looking back, she realised he had always been a hedonist. He liked high living. Even as a schoolboy, there had been a certain flashiness as well as fleshiness about him. She recalled the amount of tuck he was always demanding and how Mildred, ever loyal, had pandered to his requests. How the poor woman would now hate to know that the boy on whom she used to dote had become a confirmed alcoholic. Although she was no fool, Joanna reflected. Probably Mildred, forever on the sidelines, and with all the extra information she was bound to have gleaned from going through the contents of Crane Lodge, knew more about the whole lot of them than anyone else.

'No luck?' Sam looked up from the diary he was reading as Joanna came back from telephoning.

'No. It seems Bernard's taking a cure for alcoholism somewhere.'

'Well, I'm not surprised. Anyway, I've got plenty of work here to keep me going for a bit. Perhaps we can have a chat if and when he becomes a reformed character. There's quite a lot of other people I'd like to talk to. Reginald's contemporaries, for instance, that is, any who are still alive. And, of course, Bertie.'

'Then why don't we pop up to Crane Lodge again next Sunday? Maybe we could take him and Mildred out to lunch, if he feels up to it. There's so little for him to look forward to.'

'You're getting quite fond of the old boy, aren't you?'

'Yes. I suppose I'm trying to make up for lost time. When I was young I was against him on principle. I've come to realise I was wrong.'

'You've become more broadminded, in fact.'

'Well, Mildred did rather hold up Reginald as some kind

of hero and I used to believe her. But I now think his travels *were* probably his way of opting out of his responsibilities at home. You could say he was pretty selfish and Gloria had a legitimate grouse. I mean, what *was* she to do, seeing that she wasn't the maternal or *hausfrau* type? She must have felt let down.'

'They both felt let down. Put it like that. But it's what often happens, isn't it? Anyway, she got a title in the end, which suited her down to the ground and why she certainly wasn't going to relinquish it to marry Bertie.'

'Poor Bertie.'

'Yes, poor Bertie. You go off and ring him and Mildred right away.'

12

Two invitations within a week, Mildred thought, as she walked down to the greenhouse to give Dan, the new gardening boy, his mid-morning cup of coffee. Usually he came to the kitchen window for it, but today she was rather thankful to have forestalled him. She could not quite explain it, but his presence made her feel uneasy. He had a habit of staring at her while he stood there drinking, so that after shutting the window she would leave whatever she was doing in the kitchen and only return when she heard him put the mug down on the back doorstep and walk away. She suspected that he was late today simply because, with the thought of Crane Lodge being sold in the not too distant future, she had given him the job of clearing out and tidying the greenhouse, where he was now probably hanging about, smoking – another good reason for going to take a look.

Mildred found that she was correct in her surmise. As she opened the door, she saw him quickly grind out a cigarette underfoot and make a pretence of stacking some empty flower-pots. He looked at her sheepishly as she handed him his coffee.

'Ta, Mum.'

She felt his eyes watching her as her own travelled round the dismal unattractive mess. Even though Dan's predecessor had not been the best of gardeners, at this time of year there had always been some semblance of order and preparation for the coming season. Now, of course, there were no plans for planting seeds but the greenhouse must, at least, Mildred thought, look presentable. It was obvious that Dan had done precious little in that direction this morning.

'It is possible that estate agents may wish to look round the premises soon,' she said to him, annoyed to find that he had now reverted to his slightly insolent, grinning manner. 'I hope you can get this place up together quickly and then tackle the front drive. Some of the trees and shrubs need cutting back and the edges trimmed. I've asked the local engineers to collect the mower for an overhaul so that it will be ready for use whenever it becomes necessary. We don't want to be caught napping when the better weather arrives.'

'Yes, Mum.' He drained his mug and handed it to her, making a great show of promptly getting down on his knees to collect some loose débris as she went out of the door. She doubted such activity would last very long.

On her way back to the house, Mildred wondered about the possibility of getting someone else to replace Dan, who had certainly not lived up to what she now realised must have been a forged reference. Yet it hardly seemed worth it. Although Hansons had taken their time over the dry rot and there were still some minor unexpected repairs to be attended to, Mildred felt these could not take all that much longer. Hugh Cory had intimated that April or May would be good months to put the house on the market, with the contents being sold *in situ* round about the same time. She herself had certainly made great strides with her part in the proceedings since Christmas, which was why she could now afford to turn her attention to the garden. Indoors, her painstaking work of the past few months was visible for all to see: empty chests of drawers and wardrobes, cardboard boxes carefully labelled, a pile of odds and ends marked 'Destroy?' with a large question mark, about which Mildred had made a mental note to ask Joanna on the coming Sunday. She was looking forward to seeing her and Bertie and Sam again, as well as going to the Jamiesons' this very evening.

Ivy and John Jamieson were an elderly couple who lived half a mile along the same road as Crane Lodge. They had never been close friends of Gloria although this, to Mildred, was hardly surprising. Her late employer had been a woman much more inclined to have acquaintances rather than friends. Mildred remembered being quite surprised when, shortly before Gloria's death, they had both called at the house after tea one evening. She had often wondered afterwards whether they had been specifically invited or had merely dropped in. They had both come to the funeral and subsequently, on the few occasions when she had met them – usually while taking Jason for a walk – they had been extremely courteous and friendly. Certainly, they had never, unlike others in the district, intimated that they had been promised anything by Gloria in her will. For this, Mildred considered them to be infinitely superior to her other neighbours.

She had met Ivy Jamieson the previous week in the local post office and Ivy had expressed the hope that she was not working too hard. On hearing that Mildred felt she had lately been making good progress, Ivy asked if she might care to come to a quiet dinner with her and her husband and a date had been fixed there and then. Mildred was looking forward to the occasion and this did much to push the problem of the unsatisfactory Dan out of her mind for the rest of the day.

Wearing the new becoming outfit she had bought at Christmas, Mildred arrived at the Jamiesons', as bidden, at a quarter to eight. She found them a charming host and hostess, their conversation easy and interesting, and she was not at first surprised when Ivy asked if there was any chance of her still being a neighbour.

'I've always liked the district,' she replied, 'so it's more than possible. I've already begun making enquiries from estate agents about little flats in Richmond.'

'But you won't remain at Crane Lodge?'

Mildred looked from one to the other of them, uncertainly. Were they thinking that she was somehow hoping to retain her accommodation there by working in some capacity for the new owners? Surely not.

'I feel the time has come for me to retire,' she said, slowly. 'It will seem strange at first, but it will be as well, perhaps, and also advisable to be nearer the shops and buses. I remember my father always advocating the necessity of anyone on their own needing the amenities of town life as they got older.'

'Oh, yes,' John Jamieson broke in. 'I can see that. A house like Crane Lodge is far too large and isolated for a woman alone. You would have to employ staff. In fact, Ivy and I have sometimes worried about your present position. It doesn't seem right, somehow. I don't even like to think of you going back there tonight by yourself. Did you bring the car?'

Mildred smiled. 'No. But I'll be quite all right. It's only a step and I've put the burglar alarm on and left Jason in charge.' She did not add that Gloria, who seemed to think she might be running out of money as she grew older, refused to go in for a less erratic security system and that Jason could hardly be looked upon as much of a house dog.

'Even so,' John Jamieson persisted. 'I wouldn't want Ivy to be left alone at Crane Lodge. We did so hope that you might stay on there, but with someone to look after you for a change.'

Mildred could only suppose that they had some erroneous idea of her financial state. Even with the greatly increased income she was expecting and all that she had been careful to save throughout her life, the idea of her stepping into Gloria's shoes was so preposterous that Mildred came to the conclusion that, for all their understanding and knowledge, the Jamiesons' own affluence had blinded them to the problems of those who were not so well off.

Adamant in refusing to allow them to drag their chauffeur out to drive her the short distance home, Mildred walked back to Crane Lodge wondering how she could best return their hospitality before the place was sold. She could not but appreciate the way they had treated her as an equal, compared to her other neighbours who, while being friendly – sometimes to the point of nosiness – invariably made her feel not altogether socially acceptable.

A wind had risen during the evening and, as she left the lighted roadway and started up the long winding drive, she began to wish that she had, after all, accepted her host and hostess's kind offer of transport. The branches of the trees and shrubs, about which she had spoken to Dan only that morning, cast moving shadows beneath a fitful moon. At the thought of the gardening boy her uneasiness increased and when, at last, she reached the porch, she was annoyed to find her hand was shaking as she searched in her handbag for her key.

It was then that she heard the sound of thudding foot-steps. She whipped round just in time to see two flying figures disappearing in the direction of the park fence. She put out an arm and steadied herself against one of the pillars, her heart pounding as if it were some caged animal trying to escape from her body. Her usual composure and common sense, for once, deserted her.

It was some minutes before she managed to take hold of herself again. Then, reason told her that whoever had been out and about on nefarious business had been dis-turbed and run away. The best thing she could possibly do would be to get inside quickly and telephone the police.

The two plain clothes detectives who arrived within minutes seemed, to Mildred, incredibly young; but they were both extremely considerate and efficient. They switched on an electric fire in the drawing-room, made her sit beside it and, while one of them started looking around, the other went into the kitchen and made her a cup of tea. Later, after both had searched the premises inside and out, she was politely questioned.

Mildred was feeling much better now and almost laughed when the slightly older of the two repeated more or less the same words which John Jamieson had uttered only a short while before. 'It's a very large house for you to be all alone in, ma'am.'

'But it won't be for much longer,' she explained. 'The place will soon be up for sale.'

'All the same, is there no one who could stop with you at nights until then? A gardener, perhaps, who might be willing just to sleep here for a couple of months?'

She wondered if he noticed her nervousness return. She fancied he did not miss much. But she managed to reply, levelly, 'I'm afraid there is only a young boy working in the garden, who I do not think would be suitable.'

How could she possibly say that she had had the strong-est impression that one of the two fleeing figures she had caught sight of was Dan?

13

She hadn't been going to tell any of them that Sunday about what had taken place the previous week. Mildred disliked fuss, especially the kind which might draw attention to herself. Yet she had felt in duty bound to mention the incident to Hugh Cory now that it had been reported to the police, who she had to admit had been extremely helpful and supportive, promising her that they would keep the premises under strict surveillance and she must telephone them at any hour of the day or the night if she was at all worried.

Hugh Cory had reacted with equal solicitude and promptness. He had said that he felt someone should stay overnight at Crane Lodge and had telephoned Joanna to this effect. The latter had then rung Mildred to say that unless some stalwart body, as she put it, could be found immediately, Sam Foster would bring a suitcase with him at the weekend and remain as a stopgap, but was Mildred sure that there was no one in the district who she thought might be prepared to keep her company until the house was sold.

Although, over the years, Mildred had made friends with various people in the area, they were mostly single women in vaguely similar circumstances to herself, from none of whom would she have dreamt of asking such a favour. Besides, as both Hugh Cory and Joanna had intimated, ideally it was some tough male who was wanted, someone who could, perhaps, sleep in the little downstairs bed-sitting-room off the kitchen which had once been occupied by a cook in those far-off more sociable days when the children had been young and Gloria and Reginald had employed a larger staff.

Harassed by the thought of possibly having to accommodate Sam Foster – however well they had got on at Christmas – besides being concerned about all the trouble she seemed to be causing, Mildred thought furiously for a while and her mind suddenly came up with the idea of approaching her own kith and kin. She knew her youngest nephew – the afterthought in the family – was at somewhat of a crossroads. He had come down from university the previous summer, adamant that he did not wish to follow in his father's and brother's footsteps and take up accountancy. This had really upset Arnold, who was inclined to come the heavy father on all his offspring. Reading between the lines of Rosie's last letter, Mildred suspected that there had been plenty of rows. The boy appeared to have been drifting in and out of jobs all the winter and his mother, always a much more lenient and sympathetic character than her husband, was obviously concerned about her ewe lamb. Might it not benefit the boy to get away from home for a while, Mildred thought. If he came to stay with her, maybe she could help him to sort himself out, keep an eye on him and find out where his real inclinations lay. Surely neither of his parents could object to that.

Nor did they. After some urgent telephoning, it seemed as if two problems were going to be solved at the same time. It was agreed that Rory would arrive at Crane Lodge the following Sunday evening.

'What's he like?' enquired Joanna, when the four of them were seated at lunch that day in a new restaurant which had just opened by the river.

'I'm not sure,' Mildred replied. 'It's so long since I've seen him. And they grow up so fast nowadays. It'll be rather nice getting to know him.'

'Well, you always were wonderful with the young. I bet you'll put him on the right road in no time. I hope he does his stuff, takes care of you. We shouldn't have left you alone in the first place. If only those damned insurance people hadn't insisted Crane Lodge had to be occupied, you might have been safely in a little home of your own by now. We've taken too much advantage, even to assuming you would care for the hopeless Jason.'

Mildred smiled. 'Well, he may not be the best of guard dogs, but he's company and we're used to each other by now.'

In the afternoon, while Sam drove Bertie back to Strand-on-the-Green, Joanna and Mildred and Jason went for a walk along the towpath. It was high tide and a cold wind whipped across the water, making the small boats moored at the side toss about in a forlorn fashion, waiting for their owners and the better weather to help them come to life again.

'D'you remember,' said Joanna, 'how you used to bring Bernard and me here on Sunday afternoons in the summer when we were small and how Bernard was always on the point of falling in and making a general nuisance of himself?'

'I remember well.' Mildred waited patiently, while a recalcitrant Jason slowly caught up with them.

'You know about Bernard at the moment, do you? I mean, what's happened, where he's gone?'

There was a pause. 'I know he's taking a health cure,' Mildred replied, guardedly, 'because Felicity said something about it when she telephoned to say she wanted to buy the second bureau bookcase at probate value.'

'Because he drinks,' said Joanna, shortly.

Again there was silence for a while. 'I thought it was possible,' came the reply. And then, 'Poor Bernard.' Mildred seemed to be speaking as if to herself.

It was just like her, Joanna thought, to pity Bernard, whereas she herself could only feel anger and contempt for him. As far as she was concerned, her brother had let the side down and yet here was someone who actually felt sorry for him. Was it because Mildred had loved his father so much or simply because she was one of those rare characters who found some good in almost anyone? What a shame Bernard had never shown any appreciation for her sterling qualities and now even wanted to deny her the extra wherewithal to end her days in reasonable comfort. Thinking of that, Joanna asked how far Mildred had got in finding a new home.

'My name is down on one or two estate agents' lists,' she replied. 'It's a little difficult not quite knowing when Crane Lodge will be sold.'

'But it would be as well not to let an opportunity slip, wouldn't it? I mean, you could take out a mortgage or start paying rent until some money comes through. Old Pemberton's a bit like a squirrel, isn't he? Although I believe all executors want to hoard the assets against all eventualities. They may be right. There's always tax problems and, of course, expenses are mounting up all the time. Now there's this question of what we're going to do with the papers when Sam has finished with them, as well as all the other stuff my father accumulated which amounts to quite a considerable archive. I think the whole lot should be given to a museum.'

'That would seem a splendid idea. The Bodleian, perhaps, do you think?'

'I don't know. The trouble is that although you and Bertie and I might fancy that, Bernard would probably object. And I understand it's the duty of an executor to obtain as much as he can for all the beneficaries. If Bernard wants the archive sold, then I'm afraid that would put paid to the rest of us trying to be magnanimous. This drink problem of his makes him all the more difficult to deal with. I can only hope this cure might make him come to his senses. Tell me, did my mother drink much more than we all suspected in later years?'

For the third time that afternoon, Mildred walked on in silence for a while. She thought of all the evenings when she had had to help Gloria upstairs, undress her, take off her make-up, sometimes returning several times during the night to make sure she was all right and hadn't fallen out of bed. Drink did such terrible things to people, took such a hold, she reflected, especially where guilt was concerned. And towards the end there had been so much more than just drink: hormone injections, face lifts, slimming-pills, vitamin pills and a terrifying range of sleeping-pills. She could recall when she started to find little caches of the latter all over the house. She had spoken to Gloria's doctor about it and he had limited the amount on each prescription, telling Mildred to keep them under lock and key, not that she needed to be told. He seemed to think Gloria was a sad case and Mildred could only do her best.

She suspected that her employer had taken more than she should have on the night she died. Only that morning Mildred had come across an envelope containing twenty old Seconal tablets hidden down the side of an armchair in Gloria's bedroom. She had immediately thrown them down the lavatory, but she had come to realise that Gloria's ingenuity about such matters was limitless. After her death, Mildred had tormented herself that it might have been avoided had she gone along to her bedroom a third time to see if all was well – or as well as it ever could be. When she had confided her fears to the doctor he had assured her that she had been in no way to blame. He had been expecting Gloria's demise for some time and was not at all surprised. The death certificate stated 'Cardiac Arrest'. Looking back, Mildred wished she had taken Joanna into her confidence about it all instead of trying, as she had always done, to protect Gloria's image. It made it so much more difficult now to answer her daughter's questions honestly.

'Your mother's troubles became increasingly severe,' Mildred said, at length. 'She had been . . . unhappy for a long time.'

'Because she hated growing old?'

'Yes. And maybe other things.'

'Such as?'

Again Mildred paused. 'I think she had certain . . . regrets. Do you think we should be turning back now? We've given Bertie and Sam a nice long time together.'

Joanna knew when to take a hint. They retraced their steps, reaching Strand-on-the-Green soon after four thirty, where Mrs Pardoe had tea waiting.

Later that evening, after she had said goodbye to Sam and Joanna, Mildred went into what she now thought of as Rory's room to make sure that she had not forgotten anything. It was quite comfortable, she thought, considering that the house was obviously being dismantled. She had put a pile of books and a reading lamp beside his bed, and hung coat-hangers behind the curtain in the corner. She had even toyed that morning with the idea of putting some early daffodils from the garden in a vase on the dressing-table, but then had thought better of it. If Rory had been a girl she would not have hesitated, but he was such an unknown quantity. He might be the sort of young man who would not appreciate such a gesture.

It was getting on for nine before she heard a car coming up the drive. She went to a side window and peered out. It was a taxi all right, but not the usual kind she herself occasionally hired from the station when her car had been in dock. She saw a fair-haired bearded young man get out and come running up the steps. Quickly, she went to the door to welcome him.

'Oh, Milly,' were Rory's first words. 'Have you got twenty pounds? I didn't reckon on the transport this end being so expensive.'

'*Twenty?*' She looked at him uncertainly. 'From Richmond?'

'God, no. I took a taxi straight from King's Cross.'

14

Bernard was taking himself for a walk. He had never done such a thing before in his life. True, he had been taken for plenty of walks: by Mildred when he was small, by his schoolmasters when he was older and, sometimes, when he couldn't get out of it, by casual acquaintances at country houses where he and Felicity might be spending the weekend. But being taken and taking oneself were two entirely different matters.

Going for a walk was, to Bernard's way of thinking, the most boring and useless activity imaginable. He could remember several occasions in recent years when he had been forced to accompany some male house-guest along muddy lanes in various parts of Britain and how such characters, who had appeared to be quite witty and amusing conversationalists indoors, suddenly became more or less moronic outside, plodding along while they kept pointing out dismal things such as notices, repeating in a kind of parrot fashion: *Trespassers Will Be Prosecuted* or *Private Road to Foresters Farm*, and then relapsing into silence until some equally banal road sign like *Temporary Surface* came into view. It seemed to Bernard as if once their legs were set in motion, these walk addicts lost all sense of brain-power.

Today, dressed in brogue shoes and Burberry and carrying an umbrella – a sure indication that Bernard was not, nor ever had been, a true countryman – he set out from the Silbury Grange Clinic thinking he might only go a little way. It wasn't until he saw the spire of a village church that he changed his mind – or so he reasoned. He told himself that the idea which had just come into his head was entirely unpremeditated, that he had no intention of putting it into practice and he was going for a walk solely because he wanted to get away from the confines of the clinic and the close proximity of his fellow sufferers therein.

But with every step he took the idea seemed to take hold and become more and more attractive. He realised that he wouldn't be able to act on it, so to speak, near home base.

He would have to go further afield. He looked at his watch. Another hour to opening time. And there was the problem of getting back for lunch. It was like being at boarding-school again. He fancied the white-haired Sister-in-Charge had looked at him in a rather speculative way when he had said he was going out, reminding him that although it was Sunday and there were no exercise classes, it would be as well not to go too far and she would look forward to seeing him again at one o'clock. Did she have a sixth sense, he now wondered, about patients who might flout the rules, went after the odd snifter?

But he reckoned he was an old hand at that sort of thing. He had had many an escapade at Harrow and got away with it. He was sure he knew exactly what to do this morning. He had a fairly good idea of the lie of the land, for he had studied a map of the place before his arrival. He would make for the nearest town. There was anonymity in towns, as well as taxis. He would need transport back to the clinic if he was to return there by one.

After a few more minutes' deliberation, Bernard began walking with a will. He had a destination, a goal in sight. He had been through hell the last few weeks. He deserved a little treat. He would be able to prove to himself that he could take it or leave it. He was not to know that countless other men and women such as he had trod the selfsame paths with the selfsame ideas ever since Silbury Grange had been turned into a rehabilitation clinic; nor that the wife of a farm-worker in one of the cottages along his route shouted out to her husband as he passed, 'There's another of them on-the-wagon-chaps just gone by. City bloke by all appearances. Just put his umbrella up.'

An hour or so later, seated in the White Lion, with the welcome warmth of a double whisky slipping down his throat, Bernard felt suddenly almost human again. When he had finished it he would ask the barman to ring for a hired car. He certainly wouldn't have a second drink. This was a good test. When he got back to the clinic he would telephone Felicity and tell her to come and fetch him this very evening. He was going to discharge himself. His troubles were in the past. He was a reformed character.

Bernard looked happily around him and all but drained his glass.

The place was filling up now and a cheerful rather horsy type of man asked if he could share his table. Feeling uncommonly affable, Bernard signalled him to sit down and could not but nod in agreement when his companion raised his tankard of ale and said, 'Cheers. I always say a little bit of what you fancy does you good.'

The conversation progressed. Bernard felt it was almost incumbent on him to buy his new acquaintance, as well as himself, another drink. To hell with abstinence, he thought, as he returned to the table. The fellow was right. A little bit of what one fancied did one a hell of a lot of good.

Three double whiskies and two pints later, Bernard's drinking companion – who he had discovered was called Chuck – began to worry about him.

'You from round here?' he hazarded.

'Lunnon,' Bernard slurred, cheerfully.

'You driving?'

'No.' The bar started to tilt a little, the barman's head was definitely revolving. Bernard was quite glad to think he did not have to take the wheel.

'How you getting back?' To give him his due, Chuck, who appeared completely sober, also seemed to have some sort of conscience.

'Not going back,' said Bernard. 'Going to Shilbury Grangsh.'

'*Silbury Grange?*' Chuck became all at once on the alert. 'That's the clinic, isn't it?'

'S'right,' replied Bernard.

'I'll take you.' Chuck stood up, firmly.

'Jolly nice of you, old man.'

Chuck then armed Bernard, not without difficulty, out of the White Lion and into his waiting car, where his passenger promptly slumped down in his seat and went to sleep. When they arrived at Silbury, it seemed as if the authorities were on the look-out for their recalcitrant patient. A porter came swiftly down the steps and Bernard, now truculent and having to be supported by a man on either side of him, made an unsteady and undignified re-entry through the front door.

The Sister-in-Charge did not come to Bernard's room until the evening, by which time he had slept off the worst excesses of the morning. She was neither shocked, nor recriminatory, but obviously grieved.

'I feel we have failed, Mr Rayner,' she said, as Bernard looked at her, somewhat sheepishly, from the bed on which he was still lying. 'I had hopes that here you might have learnt that there are no half-measures with a problem such as yours. I was concerned about your going for a walk, but it is sometimes as well for patients to find out for themselves whether or not they can resist temptation. Should you wish to continue to stay with us we shall, of course, do our best to help you. But the decision must be yours. It is the necessity of admitting one is an alcoholic and the earnest *desire* to be cured which is paramount. Perhaps you would like to talk it over with your wife. I believe she is due to visit you tomorrow?'

When Felicity arrived the following day, Bernard knew exactly what he was going to do. He had already packed. He had had enough of the Silbury Clinic. There was no point in staying any longer. Remaining teetotal for the rest of his life – because that was what the Sister had implied – was not for him. He would go to the devil in his own way. Besides, he still reckoned that if he could limit himself to a certain amount of alcohol every day, it wouldn't have the catastrophic effect on him which his recent indulgence, owing to abstinence, had done. It was actually not drinking at all which had done the harm.

Felicity was furious when she heard of his intentions. She accused him of deceitfulness, cowardice and complete lack of will-power. She said that George would soon be home for the Easter holidays and she did not want the boy exposed to a sozzled stepfather. She added that she had always known Bernard was a man who, given an inch, would take more than a mile. All that had happened yesterday – about which the Sister had given her a full account – was but a case in point.

Bernard, still hung-over and bad-tempered, sat in front

of her, glowering. Then, realising that she might well drive away without him, he became more conciliatory, admitting that he had been foolish but, on reflection, he believed his slight lapse might have been all for the best. He could see where he had gone wrong. He would not completely abstain from drinking, but he vowed he would limit it to a couple of whiskies a night and no more. He then went on to suggest that perhaps they should both go away together for a little while before George came home. He had heard of an excellent establishment near Bath which, unlike Silbury, was run on the lines of a first-class hotel while giving special attention to the health of its clientele. One of the patients at Silbury had told him his wife was there at the moment, enjoying facials and massage and all sorts of rejuvenating treatments which Bernard felt sure Felicity would appreciate.

What was more, he added on seeing her weakening, being near Bath they could both take the waters . . .

15

Mildred was having unprecedented problems. Having got rid of one unsatisfactory teenager – for there had been no sign of Dan ever since the evening she had visited the Jamiesons, which made her more than ever convinced he had been one of the figures whom she had seen fleeing the grounds of Crane Lodge – she was now faced with another young ne'er-do-well, Rory. But whereas the former was simply an uncouth dim-witted layabout, her nephew was a completely different character to deal with and, what made it all the more distressing, he was a close relation.

Rory was good-looking, possessed of enormous charm and obviously extremely intelligent. Mildred had to admit that at first she had found his conversation amusing and his presence in the house stimulating – that is, when he was actually there, which wasn't often. He appeared to have a driving-licence and she had a car or, rather, the use of her late employer's Mini. In no time at all, Rory seemed to have appropriated this and, from what she could gather, had joined up with a group of like-minded young things in Richmond, all keen on the theatre.

Far from his providing company and lending support to Mildred at night, she found herself lying awake into the small hours listening not so much for intruders as for Rory's return, which might be anything up to two, three or four a.m. Once he had not come back at all and she had been on the point of ringing the police station yet again when he had turned up, full of profuse and charming apologies about running out of petrol and not wanting to disturb her beauty sleep. On being questioned as to where he had actually spent the night, he had said a friend in Chiswick had taken pity on him.

Mildred had never been a woman to be easily put out, but now she began to feel constantly anxious and angry, not only angry with her nephew but with herself and the whole wretched business of clearing up the Rayner estate. She even, on occasions, experienced a certain resentment

against both Gloria and Reginald for leaving such an un-
holy mess behind them; for just when she thought she
was coming to the end of her task, she discovered that the
cellars, which she had assumed held not much more than
a few empty trunks and rusty unidentifiable implements
– all of which could go for scrap – did, in fact, contain five
metal trunks full of more papers, maps and, to her acute
embarrassment, countless packets of old contraceptives.
She supposed she could parcel up the latter and dispose
of them in the black plastic bags that she was forever
putting out for the dustmen although, so distasteful was
her latest discovery, she felt that what she would really
like to happen would be for someone to build a bonfire on
which she, personally, could have watched them go up in
smoke when no one else was looking.

But Mildred knew that there was no question of anyone
building a bonfire at the moment. She had made tentative
hints to Rory on the subject of tending the garden, but his
response had not been encouraging. He had simply said
that although he might just be able to work the lawn-
mower – now safely back from its overhaul – he really
didn't know a weed from a wallflower and she would do
better to get in what he referred to as 'some of those
professional green-fingered wallahs – after all, I imagine
the estate could afford it'. This remark had greatly offended
Mildred. She had become so incensed that she had had to
go out of the room to cool down. Now, with the latest
revelations in the cellar, she had a sudden desire to be shot
of all her responsibilities and be settled in some little
flat of her own, where she vowed she would keep her
possessions down to a minimum, so that none of them
would hang like a mill-stone round someone else's neck
after she herself had passed on.

When she was not feeling enraged by Rory, his feckless-
ness and irresponsibility simply grieved her. Something
had to be done about the boy if he was not to turn into a
complete drifter. Why on earth had he been allowed to
develop in the way he had? Were Rosie and Arnold expecting her to work wonders where they themselves had
failed? It seemed terrible that the boy was so casual about

money that out of the cheques which they sent her for his keep they asked her to pass him a little cash weekly as, presumably, any larger sums would slip through his fingers in no time. Whatever would he do with the legacy which she had designated should come to him and his brother and sister after her death? He was continually asking her for a loan which he conveniently forgot to repay. Once or twice she had attempted to deduct these amounts from his so-called pocket-money, only to be met with, 'Oh, Milly dear, do I *really* owe you that? I did fill up with petrol yesterday, remember,' or some such other excuse. The one about the car was particularly annoying, considering how much he used it compared to her.

Mildred would have liked to have a heart-to-heart with his parents about it all. It was a difficult subject to raise on the telephone or to put into a letter. She fancied Arnold's authoritarian manner might have a lot to do with the trouble. Yet the other two children were all right, weren't they? Not for the first time did Mildred ponder the eternal question of how much nature or nurture was responsible for forming an individual's character.

It was towards the end of March when she received the worst shock of all concerning her nephew. Quite often Rory did not surface until mid-day, when he would appear in the kitchen, ravenous for whatever she had put out for him. (Mildred had early on decided it was better not to wait on him in any way.) On this particular day she had been showing an old-age pensioner round the garden, a nice old man who the Jamiesons felt might come to her rescue and keep the place reasonably tidy until any sale took place. On coming indoors again, she had found two young men in the kitchen: a dark gipsy-looking fellow, with a beard and an earring in one ear, sitting at the table, while her nephew, with his back towards her, seemed to be inspecting the contents of the refrigerator. Rory wheeled round at her entrance, his face lighting up in that devastatingly engaging way of his, as if she were the one person in the world he wanted to see.

'Ah, Milly dear. Can I introduce you to Piers? I brought

him home here for the night after he missed the last bus back to Islington.'

To give him his due, Piers then stood up, quite politely, and held out his hand. There seemed nothing else to do but take it, although she did so with misgiving.

'Where,' she asked, 'did you sleep?'

Was there, Mildred wondered afterwards, an exchange of glances between the two young men before Rory said, quickly, 'Oh, Piers is used to dossing down anywhere, Milly. But as a matter of fact, that bed you provided for me is blissfully comfortable and quite large enough for two.'

A sudden feeling of horror swept over her. So *that* was the real problem with Rory, was it? Were his parents aware? Not Arnold, surely, or he would never have foisted him on to her. Horror now mingled with disgust. Her nephew was . . . Oddly enough, a far stronger word than that usually used by the media came into her mind, only to add to her wretchedness. Her colour mounted, but her next words could have left no doubt in anyone's mind that she meant what she said.

'There must be no other occasions such as this, Rory. You came here on the understanding that you would be of help to me until this place was sold, not to stay out until all hours, use my car and bring back uninvited guests. And speaking of the car,' she added, as she moved almost regally towards the door, 'I shall be needing it myself this afternoon, so perhaps you would make other arrangements for your friend's departure.'

Once back in her own quarters, Mildred was astounded to think she had behaved in such an uncharacteristic fashion. Yet, though inwardly shaking, she was glad. It had been a straightforward instinctive gut reaction to a situation which had been thrust upon her through no fault of her own, unless she could count on being stupid enough to believe that some young nephew, whom she scarcely knew, could possibly be of use to her or, rather, the estate. For, left alone, she knew she would have preferred to forget about the Dan episode and battle on by herself for the remaining months of her custodianship of Crane Lodge.

At the moment, of course, her immediate concern was to get away for the day, to abide, in other words, by what she had told Rory even if it had been a tiny white lie. She had said she needed the car and therefore she must go somewhere. Anywhere. She would drive into Richmond and take herself out to lunch, that is, if she felt like eating anything. Then she would go for a walk. Why, she could even call on Bertie, for she still had a couple of letters of his which had fallen out from between the pages of an Ethel M. Dell novel when she had been searching through some bookshelves for reading matter to put into Rory's room. Yes, a visit to Bertie might well take her mind off things for a while, not that she would dream of telling him what was troubling her. But it would certainly help to keep her away from Crane Lodge until the evening when, please God, Rory and his gipsy lover would have made themselves scarce. She would simply have to leave it to chance as to whether they locked up properly in her absence. Stuffing the letters into an envelope, she put on her hat and coat, gathered Jason in her arms and made a swift departure.

It seemed a long tedious day. Realising that Bertie would probably need a fairly good rest in the afternoons, she did not think she should arrive at Strand-on-the-Green until well after three, by which time her mind had come up with several courses of action to take over the problem of Rory, only to reject each one in turn. The overriding hideous thought from which she could not escape was whether the boy might possibly have, or at least be a candidate for, Aids. Should she have a complete show-down with him? Send him home? Get his parents to come south? Was there no hope that he would ever lead a normal life? The devastating thing about it all was that he seemed so *happy*. So *gay*, in fact, Mildred thought grimly as, with Jason at her heels, she trudged along the towpath, painfully aware that she was an ageing spinster, alone and completely out of her depth. I have outlived my time, she thought, as she arrived at Bertie's yellow-painted front door.

He himself was also feeling extremely low that afternoon, so that the sight of Mildred being ushered into his sitting-room by Mrs Pardoe was more than welcome.

At first, he thought she might have called to see him about the letter from Hugh Cory, copies of which he imagined they all would have received. His own had arrived in the mid-day post and when he heard that Mildred had not yet seen hers, he passed it over, saying, 'Looks as if we shall have to find another executor and trustee. Poor old Percy Pemberton seems to have kicked the bucket.'

16

'I was wondering,' said Hugh Cory to Joanna on the telephone, 'whether you'd consider becoming an executor and trustee of the estate now Percy Pemberton has died.'

'Oh.' Joanna was taken by surprise. 'Can I? I mean, being a beneficiary . . .'

'Why, yes. The only thing a beneficiary can't be is a witness to a will.'

'Oh.' Joanna sat down suddenly and tried to think what it might entail. She supposed it was a compliment to be asked, but she wasn't at all sure she wanted the job. Hugh hadn't mentioned anything about asking Bernard and, if she took it on, her brother would be sure to be upset. As the eldest of the family, he would feel usurped.

'Perhaps you'd like to think about it. Don't answer now,' Hugh went on kindly, 'but of course having no executor will hold things up a bit more and, in any case, we shall have to apply to the courts to appoint any new ones. It's not an easy estate to administer, as you must well realise by now. I would be willing to become a joint executor with you. Two heads are always better than one. I fear it was beginning to worry Percy no end. In fact, he had intimated to me recently that he would like to hand over to someone younger on the grounds of his health and age.'

'Oh.' That's three 'Ohs' in a row, Joanna thought. How difficult this is. Poor Percy. I wonder if we killed him off. We never took into account that there he was, old and all by himself, having to deal with such an odd will and such an odd collection of beneficiaries. No wonder the responsibility got him down. I feel I ought to support Hugh, but it would make Bernard mad.

'My brother,' she said, rather lamely, and stopped.

There was a pause on the other end of the line. 'I believe he is not at all well,' Hugh volunteered, obviously doing his best to be tactful. 'In fact, I had a telephone call from his wife the other day. She has asked me to get in touch with her direct for the time being, as she doesn't want him worried. The protracted problems concerning the estate seem to have aggravated his . . . er, condition.'

So you know, do you, Joanna thought. Or you've guessed. Neither Silbury Grange nor that place near Bath appear to have done Bernard much good. I wonder if I ought to go up to Hampstead some time and pay a sisterly call, except that I don't expect it would be appreciated. All the same, I think I will. And I could see Hugh and spend a night at Crane Lodge. I'm not happy about Mildred. She sounded most unlike her usual self the last time we spoke on the telephone. That nephew of hers was worse than useless. Apparently he's pushed off. God, when *is* this all going to end?

'Have you,' she asked, suddenly changing the subject, 'any news about the sale of the house? And the contents?'

'Yes. I was coming to that. Just before he died, Percy said he thought the house should now go on the market. There's a letter in the post about it to you all. And I have been in contact with the auctioneers about selling the contents as soon as they can organise it. As I'm sure you're aware, it is always advisable to show people round a house that is still furnished, but I shall naturally insist that any prospective viewer must be accompanied by an estate agent. I don't want Miss Treadgold inconvenienced any more than we can help. She has really done a splendid job all through the winter.'

'Yes, I quite agree. I expect you know that she's all alone again and prefers not to have any more company.'

'So I gather. I'm sorry about this. But perhaps with the lighter evenings . . .' This time Hugh Cory felt it was he who appeared inadequate and uncertain. How difficult it was to safeguard Mildred, protect the beneficiaries, pacify a belligerent Bernard and his wife and obtain the best financial deal for all concerned, while coping with several other wills at the same time. At this season of the year the obituary columns were always at their longest. Flu, pneumonia, heart disease knocked the elderly down like ninepins. The winding up of at least three more estates had come his way only that week, although he could wager that none of them would be on a par with Gloria Rayner's when it came to complications.

Hugh Cory thought how nice it would be if he could have taken a holiday, but he knew that it was no good thinking about that until August, when he hoped he and his family might spend three weeks in Wales. The most he could expect at the moment was an extra day, perhaps, tacked on to the Easter break. People always accused lawyers of spinning things out for their own ends, but if they did but know, as far as he was concerned, the sooner the Rayner estate was off his hands the better. He hoped none of his sons would want to go in for the Law. One so seldom got a thank you, although he had to admit that Joanna was an exception and Bertie Fane and Mildred were both pleasant characters. It was that fellow Bernard and his wife who really got him down. It was difficult to believe he was Joanna's brother.

He was relieved when before ending their conversation she said she would come up to London the following week and call at his office. Of the four beneficiaries, she was the only one to whom he felt able to turn under the present circumstances. Mildred and Bertie, while conscientious and intelligent, were too old and he suspected that Bernard's drink problem was getting altogether out of hand. Hugh could not help hoping that Joanna would, in the end, be the one to inherit Gloria's capital. Wearily, he picked up his pen and began jotting down the things he would like to discuss with her when she arrived.

Almost always uppermost in his mind was Percy Pemberton's concern about libel, both in respect of Sam Foster's book and the remaining archive. Personally, he did not think there was nearly the risk which Percy seemed to have had in mind. The book could be read by experts in this field before publication and, as for the other papers and letters, he felt sure the problem could be got round somehow. Nevertheless, now that the spectre had been raised, it wouldn't go away and presumably steps would have to be taken, Counsel's opinion would come into it and Counsel's opinion was invariably expensive. Now that April was coming along he, Hugh, would have to get out a statement of account. He supposed that was one of the things Bernard's wife wanted to prevent him from seeing. Certainly, Hanson's bill for attending to the dry rot had come way over the estimate, but then, of course, so many other things had turned out to need doing. As for his own firm's account, it was bound to be heavy.

Then there were so many niggling little problems which had just arisen. There were three antique swords which Mildred had recently come across in the coal cellar at Crane Lodge, labelled 'Property of General Willesdon', and she had explained that the General had passed on many years ago. Hugh had had to find out who were the deceased's solicitors and had actually been drafting a letter to them about this on the morning Percy had died, while the afternoon's post had brought two more headaches.

The new jobbing gardener whom Mildred had taken on, a Mr Brewer, had written a more or less illiterate letter from which Hugh had just been able to make out that the man did not want to be paid weekly, but would like a lump sum when his services were no longer required. It was obvious that the man was trying to fiddle his social security benefits and was after cash. Being a solicitor, Hugh could not be party of any kind of wangle like that. He would have to go into the matter and although, thank God, it was quite straightforward and nothing about which he would have to take Counsel's advice, it would still take time and time, at least to the beneficiaries, cost money.

Then Bertie had written him a charming, altogether different letter, concerning an idea which had just come to him. Was it too late, if all the beneficiaries agreed, to create some sort of bursary in favour of Reginald's old school. A scholarship bearing his name, perhaps. Something like that, which Bertie understood would save tax. Although Hugh realised that he was quite right in this assumption, it should have been thought of before and, in any case, it would surely not go down very well with Bernard, who had already objected to the idea of giving away the archive. Nevertheless, he would raise the question with Joanna when she came to see him.

One of the telephones on his desk suddenly rang and

he picked up the receiver. Was it too much to hope that, for once, it wasn't bad news? Yet, as soon as he heard his secretary say, 'Miss Treadgold is on the line, sir,' he feared the worst. Mildred never rang unnecessarily. She usually communicated in neatly typed, well thought-out letters, for which he was grateful.

'She said she didn't want to bother you, sir,' the girl went on, 'but there's been a bit of an accident.'

'Accident?' Hugh was immediately on the alert, all weariness pushed aside. 'Is she hurt?'

'Oh, no sir. It's not Miss Treadgold. It's the new gardener, Mr Brewer. Apparently he . . .'

Hugh cut her short. 'Put Miss Treadgold straight through, will you, Elaine.'

Mildred sounded more distressed than he had ever known her. Her calm sensible manner seemed to have given way to hysteria. 'Mr Brewer was making a bonfire, Mr Cory,' she burst out. 'On my instructions. I feel so awful about it. He couldn't get it to light properly. We had a little rain in the night, didn't we? So he . . . used *petrol*, Mr Cory. There was an explosion. I got an ambulance and went with him to Queen Mary's Hospital.'

'How badly is he hurt?' Hugh's normally quiet pleasant voice was harsh now.

'I'm not sure, Mr Cory. I did what I could with cold water while we were waiting for the ambulance. One of his hands . . . his chin . . . I feel so responsible. You see, I *asked* him to make the bonfire.'

'But not to use petrol, surely?'

'Oh, no. I suppose he got it from the spare can I keep hidden in the garage. Actually, I thought it was empty after my nephew left. He would keep finding where I'd put it and using it all up. But . . . oh, Mr Cory . . .' Mildred seemed to be crying now. 'Mrs Brewer's been on to me. She said something about suing the estate.'

'Miss Treadgold, please.' Hugh did his best to pacify her, although the mention of suing jarred on his already overstrained nerves. 'You must not blame yourself. Things may not be as bad as you think. Leave it with me. I should like to be informed of Mr Brewer's condition when you next telephone Queen Mary's. Meanwhile, try not to worry. I've just been speaking to Mrs Lawson and she intends to visit you next week. She is always so helpful. We must all hope for the best.'

After Hugh had replaced the receiver, he sat for quite a while with his head in his hands. *Try not to worry. We must all hope for the best.* Platitudes. Yet what else could he do or say at the present moment? But if there was one thing about which he was quite certain, it was that there was a jinx on the Rayner estate. An action against it was all that was needed – or, rather not needed.

And what the hell would happen if the old boy's wife *did* decide to bring one?

17

Contrary to expectations, Felicity did not seem at all averse to Joanna paying her and Bernard a visit when she suggested it on the telephone that evening. In fact, it seemed almost as if her sister-in-law welcomed the idea. Of course, Joanna knew that Felicity was unpredictable. Just when one was ready for a rebuff, she often became affable in the extreme. Yet usually there was some obscure reason behind such behaviour, which did not become manifest until later on.

Joanna had decided to spend at least two nights at Crane Lodge because, since speaking to Hugh Cory that morning, so many more problems had cropped up, not the least being the gardener's accident about which Mildred appeared to be consumed with self-reproach; although, as far as Joanna could gather, it had now turned out that Mr Brewer had actually brought his own petrol to ignite the bonfire and his burns were not as serious as had been thought. Though naturally sorry for the old man, Joanna was relieved to think it was unlikely that any case could or would be brought against the estate. But Mildred was obviously very worked up about it.

As her train drew into Waterloo the following week, Joanna hoped she might be able to give Mildred a little moral support. Her agitation was, she supposed, understandable. Mildred was getting on and she had had such a hell of a time the last winter. Apart from the thankless task of clearing up such a ghastly mess as Crane Lodge, there had been that horrible shemozzle over George's friend, Tim, at Christmas; then an attempted break-in; the unfortunate episode with her ne'er-do-well nephew (although Mildred had been extremely cagey as to what form his worthlessness took); her growing awareness of Bernard's 'illness', as she now called it; and lastly old Mr Brewer nearly blowing himself up at her behest.

Joanna felt it was a good thing she would be spending a little time quietly with Mildred alone, especially as Sam seemed more than happy to be left to get on with his book, over which he was becoming completely obsessed. Besides, she was much happier about leaving the shop nowadays, having at last found a girl capable of taking charge in her absence, who had promised to contact Sam in case of any untoward difficulties.

Leaving her suitcase at the station, Joanna made her way straight to Hampstead where she was expected for lunch. Aware that the Easter holidays had not yet started, she was surprised when George answered the door to her, although he quickly explained that he had been sent home early due to illness.

'So ridiculous,' Felicity said, as she came out of the drawing-room into the hall. 'It seems to me that all they do at that school is duck out of their responsibilities. George had flu rather badly and the authorities thought he would do better to recuperate here. Now, let him take your coat upstairs and come on in and have a drink.'

Leading the way, she continued, over her shoulder, 'Bernard, believe it or not, has actually gone to see a friend who's trying to persuade him to join Alcoholics Anonymous. I can't think this chap will succeed, but anything's worth a try. The bore is, though, that whichever way the problem's tackled, I feel I can only drink surreptitiously whenever the opportunity presents itself. Let's make the most of this one. What would you like?'

When Felicity had poured them each a large gin and tonic, she went on, 'Bernard's retired from the City. Did you know? Of course, what really happened was that his firm *asked* him to retire. It's an appalling situation. God knows where we'll be financially. There don't seem to be any hand-outs coming from the estate yet and, even when there are, Bernard thinks they'll only amount to a pittance. I blame Gloria for all his trouble. That's why I've taken over dealing with these wretched solicitors' letters at the moment. Never-ending, aren't they? Copies here, there and everywhere. I can't understand *how* Gloria was ever allowed to make such a balls-up in the first place. Forgive me. I know she was your mother, too.'

Joanna sipped her drink, waiting for the tirade to end. By the time it did, she had actually begun to feel sorry for her brother and sister-in-law. She had known that Bernard had always been a heavy drinker, but she could quite see how and why this state of affairs had been exacerbated.

'When the house and contents are sold,' she said, hopefully, 'the tax position will be a little clearer. Then the trust can be set up and we'll all probably be getting more than you think. Hugh asked me if I would consider becoming a joint executor and trustee with him, now that Percy has died. But I don't think that would be a good idea, do you? I'd like to help but it might upset Bernard even more. I thought I'd just mention this, as I'm going to see Hugh later on today.'

'Nice of you to think like that.' Felicity became quite conciliatory. 'But I agree it would just about finish Bernard. He already feels he's being treated like a child. Mind you, at the moment he's acting like one. It's not a happy household. That's something else I want to talk to you about or, rather, ask you. It may seem awful cheek but . . . it's this business of George being sent back early from school. I'd already got him fixed up to spend most of the holidays with the families of his friends, but it's this interim period that's bothering me. The atmosphere here isn't good for him. I wonder if you'd consider taking the child back with you to the country for a fortnight?'

So *that* was why Felicity had been so keen to see her, was it? Joanna felt furious. Besides, it was no small order to be asked to accommodate a boy of George's age, not with the kind of life she led. She was about to say something to this effect when a car drew up at the front door bringing Bernard home.

'We'll talk later,' said Felicity, quickly. Making some excuse about seeing if lunch was ready, she left the room.

Joanna was shocked at the change in her brother since she had last seen him. He seemed an old man. His face, admittedly no longer florid, had an unhealthy pallor, the flesh hanging in folds on either side of his nose and mouth. She thought he looked like a morose Saint Bernard, and then felt guilty for the unfortunate comparison. He greeted her in an off-hand way and, during the ensuing meal, remained taciturn and moody. Most of his attention seemed to be focused on George, whom he castigated for bad table manners, leaving food on his plate and not having had his hair cut. Joanna could quite see why Felicity wanted her son out of the way.

After lunch Bernard shuffled off in the direction of his study and Joanna felt all she could do was to return to the unresolved question of having George to stay with her. Despite her initial anger at Felicity's deviousness, having just witnessed her brother's behaviour towards the child, it seemed churlish to refuse. Yet she could think up plenty of reasons for doing so. The boy's mother had, however, evidently anticipated these.

'He's awfully good at looking after himself, Jo. He's a quiet child. Not a bit like that little horror we had at Christmas. George would never do anything like that. He's bookish. He'd love your shop. I don't think he'd be any trouble and the country air is just what he needs. Besides, you saw how Bernard treated him at lunch. I'd be so grateful if you'd have the kid.'

For Felicity actually to express gratitude was certainly something, thought Joanna. And she obviously *was* in a hole. Having George to stay in her flat above the bookshop would be inconvenient, but it wouldn't exactly kill her. And Bernard, for all his boorish ways, *was* her brother and Felicity her sister-in-law, even if this small rather pathetic child hardly seemed to belong to either of them. But that, of course, was all the more reason for doing him a kindness. Before leaving, Joanna found herself arranging to meet George and his mother at Waterloo in two days' time.

It wasn't until she was upstairs putting on her coat in Felicity's bedroom that Joanna happened to catch sight of the small carriage clock beside her bed. She recognised it at once. It was a pretty, unusual piece which she believed to be valuable and had always stood on the desk in her father's study. So far as she could remember, it had never worked properly and she had not actually noticed it there since his death. Now, it was ticking away and showing the correct time. She was instantly reminded of an afternoon back in the previous autumn, when she had come downstairs with Mildred to see Felicity hastily zipping up a small hold-all.

All the anger which Joanna had felt before lunch returned, but with far greater intensity. Her sister-in-law must have nicked it, relying on Mildred's loyalty, especially to Bernard, not to say anything. Joanna was debating whether now to make an issue of it herself, when she heard a step behind her and Felicity came into the room.

'I suppose you're looking at the clock,' she said, defensively. 'Gloria always said I could have it when she died. As you know, she never bothered to specify anything like this in her will, but she was quite insistent about it, just as she was about my having her latest mink. I certainly didn't want *that*. Bernard had just bought me one and I wouldn't dream of wearing second-hand clothes, anyway. But the clock was different. It was lying in a drawer and in need of repair. I saw no harm in taking it. There was no point in it being sold along with all those other things, or ear-marking it to buy at probate value when it was definitely *promised*. Bernard quite agreed. He said it would be something to remember his father by. Of course, we both think that Gloria meant me to have her jewellery, if only she'd got round to updating her will.'

'Yes, I see.' But Joanna did not really see. She only saw that, between them, Bernard and Felicity had been dishonest and she wondered what else they might have appropriated or, perhaps, not to put too fine a point on it, pinched.

Quickly, she thanked her sister-in-law for lunch, confirmed that she would meet her and George at Waterloo in two days' time, and left.

18

Sam Foster studied Reginald Rayner's diary for 1932 once again. He often found himself coming back to it: the year when his subject had spent so much time abroad. Reginald appeared to have gone to Egypt in the early spring, returned to England because of illness for a brief spell in June and then disappeared to Borneo, where he remained until November. Joanna was born the following March.

It was possible, Sam thought, that she had been conceived by Gloria and Reginald the previous summer. Possible, but not probable, not after what Mildred had told him last Christmas. She had said that Lady Rayner never liked to miss the London season. Here, Mildred had actually volunteered some extra information about Gloria being pleased that both her children had been March babies so that she was able to get her figure back in time for her most important round of social activities: Ascot, Wimbledon, Henley. Mildred had gone on to say that Sir Reginald hated all that kind of thing so much that he always welcomed any excuse to get out of it, having once found a bad dose of gippy tummy preferable to escorting his wife to Gold Cup Day. When Sam had quickly asked, 'Which year was that?', Mildred had replied, equally promptly, '1932.'

Had she gone a shade pinker when she had said that? Sam fancied that she had.

If Reginald had been as ill as Mildred made out, it would seem doubtful that he had engaged in any form of sexual activity at that time. Gloria, by then, had taken up with Bertie who, if not yet suspected of being her lover, was nevertheless a constant escort of whom, presumably, Reginald approved; or, at least, one whom he accepted as someone who could conveniently relieve him of his own husbandly duties. Sam knew it was an era when such situations were a great deal more common than people imagined.

The more he thought about this, the more convinced he became that he was right in his surmise. Joanna was not Reginald's daughter. Judging by photographs of him, it would seem that while Bernard definitely had his father's build and heavy jowls, Joanna bore no resemblance to him at all, nor, strangely enough – apart from her large blue and much more friendly eyes – to Gloria or, for that matter, to Bertie. Except for one thing which Sam had noticed last Christmas. It was a mannerism: the way she lifted her hand to her chin and held it there when she was concentrating. Bertie had done exactly the same when they had all been in the drawing-room at Crane Lodge listening to the Queen's speech before that fool of a boy had got out on the roof. Sam realised it was a common enough gesture. Nevertheless, he had been particularly struck by it.

Surely the question of her paternity must have crossed Joanna's mind. Had she just preferred to ignore it? He was well aware how many individuals were able to suppress unwelcome thoughts, burying them so deeply in the subconscious that it was as if they had never surfaced. But the very fact that she so often referred to Reginald by his Christian name and not 'my father' made Sam all the more certain that she was not merely suffering from a blind spot. She was too straightforward an individual for that.

Had brother and sister ever talked about it, Sam wondered? Bernard, of course, had never really accepted Bertie. Maybe, he preferred to ignore the possibility that he was Joanna's father, merely for the sake of propriety. Bernard was all for that, even though he was now letting the side down badly over his unfortunate addiction to alcohol. Sam could not believe that Bernard would ever have had his sister's personal feelings at heart. He would simply have kept his suspicions to himself. As for Mildred, she was so constituted that, even if she had always known more than either of them, she would also have kept her own counsel, deeming it wisest to let the secret go down with her to the grave.

Bertie was the person with the real answers, Sam mused. But one couldn't possibly ask him. It was unthinkable. He was old and sick. Besides, if Joanna truly hadn't suspected anything, it would be criminal to raise the question. Even if one was working on the life of someone who was dead, there were some things best left alone for the sake of those still living.

All the same, the journalist in Sam kept nagging away at the problem. It fascinated him. He found himself constantly speculating as to whether it was possible that Gloria, at the height of her beauty, cold, casual but avid for men's attention, had actually allowed both Reginald and Bertie to sleep with her that summer so that either of them could, in fact, have been Joanna's father. Sam was hazy about when paternity tests had come into being. But even if that method of confirmation had been available, it was hardly likely that Gloria would have gone in for it. She would have kept quiet, very quiet. As Sam supposed he would have to do now.

Still, it was interesting, so interesting that when he spoke to Joanna on the telephone the first evening she was away, he knew how difficult it would be to keep his suspicions to himself when she returned. However, as soon as he heard that she would be bringing George back with her in two days' time, his mind switched immediately to more practical matters. It seemed obvious that Joanna had been taken advantage of and he told her so in no uncertain terms.

'You can't, Jo. It isn't as if you're a lady of leisure. Bernard and Felicity had no right to ask you.'

'It wasn't Bernard. It was Felicity. And I'm doing it for the child's sake, not theirs.'

'But he's not your nephew. He's your sister-in-law's son by another man.'

'Yes, I know. But I'm sorry for him. Bernard's a sad case and he's picking on the kid. It'll only be for a fortnight and then he's going off to stay with friends. Anyway, I've promised, so there it is.'

As they rang off, Joanna wondered if she would ever have made the promise if she had found out about the clock earlier. She hoped she would not have allowed her moral indignation to stand in the way of her inherent compassion towards the underdog.

Naturally, she had decided to say nothing to Sam or anyone else about her brother and sister-in-law's unscrupulousness. It was, in any case, something she fully intended to try to forget and, just at the moment, she was finding this easier than expected, having been faced, ever since her arrival at Crane Lodge, with a distraught Mildred who seemed unable to talk about anything other than Mr Brewer and his accident. Joanna had never seen her in such a state. On pointing out that it had been a perfectly reasonable job to have asked a gardener to undertake, Mildred kept saying that she had been far too insistent on it being done quickly, that it could have waited until drier conditions, that the poor man was only trying to please her and she would never forgive herself. She even talked wildly of wanting to buy him a new television set as a compensatory present, which made Joanna wonder whether the strain of the past months, coupled with the prospect of increased wealth, had made her temporarily unhinged.

Joanna found it quite a relief, next day, to visit Bertie who was, as usual, delighted to see her. She brought him up to date regarding her discussion with Hugh, thanked him for his idea of creating a bursary for Reginald's old school of which she herself was all in favour, while explaining, however, that Bernard's persistent non-co-operative attitude was making everything so difficult that she had decided she was unable to take on the job of executorship. Finally, she touched on Mildred's extraordinary behaviour concerning the bonfire.

'Could be,' Bertie said, after hearing her out, 'that she had something confidential she wanted to burn.'

'Confidential?' Joanna frowned. 'I can't think what. Mildred would never get rid of anything to do with the estate without . . . well, consulting Hugh or one or the other of us. No, I can't believe that. Anyway, what are refuse collectors for?'

Bertie thought about the packets of letters which Mildred had kept passing him. He could understand someone wanting personally to see to the disposal of something. He was quite sure Mildred would not do anything underhand. No, she must have found some bit of evidence detrimental, say, to a member of the family. Reginald, most likely.

Bertie had always been aware of her feelings towards him.

'I shouldn't worry too much, Jo,' he said, at length. 'We all know Mildred is the soul of honesty. We've put our trust in her to clear up Crane Lodge and she's done a magnificent job. I dare say she's just overtired. Do your best to cheer her up. Let's hope the sale of the house and furniture will soon be over and things will sort themselves out. Mr Brewer wasn't badly burned, I understand.'

'No, thank God. He's talking of coming back to work in a week or so. But that's what makes Mildred's agitation all the more incomprehensible. I hope to heavens you're right about things getting sorted out. I never realised that death could cause such a hornet's nest, or perhaps Pandora's Box would be another way of putting it. Out pop the problems one after another. They may not all be unsolvable but they're so unexpected and they will keep coming. Besides, they produce others in their wake. We seem to have got Bernard an alcoholic, Mildred on the verge of a breakdown, Sam obsessed with his book and poor Hugh Cory looks as if he could do with a long, long holiday. I'm beginning to think you and I are the only ones, so far, not to be too adversely affected, if you see what I mean.'

'Yes, I do see,' he answered, and then stopped as Mrs Pardoe brought in the tea.

He asked Joanna to pour and watched as she did so, grateful for the interruption. Although, he reflected, he wasn't going to tell her now. Not yet. Better to let the growing bond between them develop a little more. Besides, if he told her one thing, he would have to mention the other. There were always two sides to every question, sometimes more.

19

'Wot you doin' 'ere?' The ginger-haired boy sitting by the duck-pond plucked at a blade of grass, put it in his mouth and began to chew, thoughtfully.

'I'm staying at the Countryside Bookshop.'

'Wot? Wiv Mrs Foster?'

George coloured. 'No. With Mrs Lawson. She's my stepfather's sister.'

The gingerhead chewed on in silence. Presently he asked. 'Why ain't you at school?'

'I've been ill. I was sent home early. It's a boarding-school.'

'Oh. You're one of them, are you? A top 'at and tails chap.'

'No,' replied George, stoically, although becoming redder and more and more uncomfortable. He wished he hadn't come out for what Joanna had said he needed, 'a breath of fresh air'. He had been helping her in the book-shop all the afternoon, where she was doing something called stock-taking. He had stood on a small step-ladder and shouted out titles to her and sometimes made lists by himself, when she was called away to speak to a customer or talk on the telephone.

George had really enjoyed himself. He loved books and reading. English was his best subject at school. He thought it might be a good thing to become a bookseller when he grew up or, better still perhaps, an author like that Foster chap. He was annoyed that this uncouth local boy had assumed that Joanna was Sam's wife. After all, they didn't live together although, since George had arrived, there had hardly seemed a day that went by without them having some sort of contact. Joanna had told George to be back by six tonight, because they would be driving over to supper with Sam. Looking at his watch, he was pleased to find it was a quarter to the hour.

'I've got to go now,' he said. 'My aunt is taking me somewhere.'

Ginger gave a smirk. 'An' I bet I know where,' he

retaliated. 'If that pair ain't married, then they oughter be, the way they carry on. It's pretty plain wot they gets up to after dark.'

George began to run. He did not want to think about what Joanna and Sam got up to after dark or, for that matter, what his mother and stepfather or anyone else got up to after dark. Or, rather, he couldn't *help* thinking about it, but he didn't like what he thought.

What he felt he would really like now would be to live somewhere with just one other person: Mildred, for instance. Joanna, nice as she was, was no good because she had the shop and this Sam person taking up so much of her time. Mildred was the only other grown-up he could think of who would be about right, even though he did not know her very well. But the best thing about her was that she did not seem to be connected with any man.

George wondered whether, when Sam and Joanna took him back to London at the coming weekend, he could ask if he could stop at Crane Lodge for a night or two until it was time to go to his friends. He really hated the Hampstead house now. Bernard frightened him and his mother always seemed so tired and scratchy. He couldn't understand why they had ever married as neither of them appeared at all happy. It would be nice, George thought, if his real father came to see him sometimes. He fantasised about this quite a bit. He was sure he wasn't a shyster or a bounder as Bernard kept calling him. He was probably some super chap who would turn up at school one day in a brand new Rolls and make the other boys green with envy. But George had long ago given up actually asking his mother about this possibility, just as he had given up asking her about a lot of far more ordinary things.

On the way over to Sam's house that evening, George plucked up courage and shyly asked Joanna whether he could stay at Crane Lodge when she took him back. She had seemed startled, but said she would see. But then she went on to say that it might be too much for Miss Treadgold and if the worst came to the worst she would keep George with her until he could go straight on to his friends. She seemed to sense that he wanted to avoid his mother and stepfather at all costs. George felt that Joanna was on his side, although it was a little disheartening when she also mentioned that she was going to be exceptionally busy in the weeks ahead, how she had to see her accountant and her bank manager. She explained that she was hoping to expand her business and perhaps go in for a few enterprises, such as promoting certain authors, getting them to come to the shop and sign their books.

In response to this, George had said, 'What if they're dead?' and she had laughed and replied, 'Well, sometimes they have descendants.' 'Like you?' George had countered, with commendable quickness of thought. 'When that book about your father comes out, you could sign that.' But Joanna had suddenly gone silent and muttered something about that wasn't possible and, in any case, it wasn't quite what she had meant. George wondered if he would ever find a grown-up who didn't have secrets and worries.

Joanna still hadn't said anything to him about staying with Mildred when Sam called for them both the following Sunday morning. All George knew was that they would be having lunch at Crane Lodge after which, he presumed, his mother would turn up to collect him. He supposed Joanna had forgotten their conversation, for she had certainly seemed very preoccupied the last few days and he hadn't liked to bring up the subject again.

Nor, when he had woken up that day, had he liked to mention how much his throat was hurting, for fear Joanna would think he was pretending to be ill so that he could stay a little longer with her. After they had heard Sam's familiar toot, George had merely followed her out to the car, climbed into the back and promptly fallen asleep.

When, a couple of hours later, he found himself being shaken awake by Sam, he still felt miserable, as well as hot, stiff-necked and unable to swallow properly. Mildred, who had come out to greet them, took one look at him and said, 'That child's got mumps.'

'Oh, my God.' He was aware of three grown-ups staring at him in consternation. 'I'd better telephone his mother,' Joanna went on. 'He won't be able to go to his friends, that's for sure.'

There followed some anxious conversation as to who or who had not had mumps. Sam volunteered cheerfully that he had had the disease as a child. So, apparently, had Mildred, but she was emphatic that neither Joanna nor Bernard had ever succumbed. To Joanna's everlasting gratitude, she then added, 'I think I'll go and make up the bed in the room Rory used. It would seem to me best if the child stays here.'

George, despite his discomfort, visibly brightened. His wish had been granted, if not quite in the way he had contemplated.

Felicity, as Joanna had expected, became practically hysterical on the telephone. 'He can't possibly come home. I've never had mumps, let alone Bernard. And it can be fatal at our age. I don't mean the usual complications, men becoming impotent and all that.' She gave a slight giggle. 'But I know someone of fifty who actually died,' she went on. 'Meningitis set in. Thank heavens Mildred says she'll cope. But, of course, she's much more in a position to do so now than any of us, isn't she? I mean, she's only got herself to think of and she's done all the spade work at Crane Lodge. It's more or less just showing people round the house now and presumably the estate agents will do that, anyway. And at least she'll have *male* company now her nephew's so mysteriously disappeared.' Felicity giggled again, somewhat helplessly, before continuing, 'Do tell her that I'll get our doctor to call. Or no, wait. Better perhaps to get the local one who dealt with Gloria. He must be used to coming to Crane Lodge. And please say Mildred must buy anything the poor child wants. Anything. Let me know the cost and I'll reimburse her. Brand's Essence might be good. It's really too bad, George having only just had flu. Why does all this have to happen to me?'

'How is my brother?' Joanna managed to break in at last.

'Bernard? You know Bernard. Some days he's sober and some days he isn't. However hard I try to keep my own supply of alcohol under lock and key he gets hold of a bottle somehow. Alcoholics do. They're so ingenious. He started inveigling my new au pair into buying him supplies. When I found out what was happening, I fired her. I've no one at the moment. So how could I have George, anyway?'

'No. I see.' Joanna recalled having made the same kind of reply to her sister-in-law not long ago. But once again, she didn't really see, any more than she did the last time. Other mothers managed didn't they, when their offspring had mumps, even if they or their husbands hadn't had it. Other mothers didn't foist their children off on to anyone who would have them. Other mothers coped, somehow.

But Felicity was not a coper. She was a spoilt avaricious woman, now fast becoming an embittered one because life hadn't worked out in the way she wanted and her mother-in-law hadn't left her a diamond necklace and earrings and hadn't made her only son her chief legatee.

20

The woman who had been brought to see Crane Lodge by the young estate agent appeared to be much more interested in Mildred than the house itself. At least, that was the impression Madame Levitte gave when, on arrival, she seemed to hang about in the hall saying, in a slightly foreign accent, 'I believe this was the home of the famous explorer, Sir Reginald Rayner?'

Mildred had merely replied that this was correct. She couldn't see why the fact should have much influence on any prospective purchaser. Mildred was even more puzzled and disconcerted when Madame Levitte went on to enquire how long she had been with the family, adding, '*Vous vous occupiez des enfants, n'est pas? Ils ont le même age que moi.*'

After the visitor had at last been persuaded to move into the drawing-room, Mildred went to see George who, happily, was well on his way to recovery and watching television in Rory's old room. She couldn't quite shake off the feeling that Madame Levitte's face was vaguely familiar. But it wasn't until after she had departed that Mildred had gone up to her own flat and stared at the photograph which had fallen out of one of Reginald's old knapsacks and which she had placed for safe keeping in a top drawer of her dressing-table. Now, she studied it again, long and hard.

The woman in the picture and the one who had just left were not one and the same. That was obvious. But the similarity was striking. The picture Mildred now held in her hand was of a shorter, thinner, dark-haired lady, eastern-looking and dressed in some kind of caftan. Was she the mother of Madame Levitte who, in certain respects, bore a strange likeness to Bernard?

Mildred sat thinking. In the back of her mind she had always thought that there must have been another woman in Reginald's life, however much it distressed her. She had a feeling that Gloria must have known too, even though she had carefully concealed the fact. Mildred had often wondered if there had been a child. Today, she felt she had the answer. That was why her visitor had asked about those other children, 'the same age as me'.

But if these suppositions were correct, what did Madame Levitte want? She did not look hard up. She was perfectly groomed, beautifully dressed. Mildred felt she had no real desire to buy Crane Lodge. That had simply been a pretext. She had wanted information about the Rayner family and had obviously been delighted to have found someone who might give it to her.

Although immensely curious, Mildred felt that this was a problem she could well have done without. In many ways, she hoped she would hear no more from Madame Levitte, but this was not to be. The following morning, about eleven o'clock, she arrived once again at Crane Lodge, this time alone. Mildred stood at the front door, surprised and somewhat hostile. If the woman wanted a second viewing, then she should have made an appointment and come with an agent.

'Forgive me.' The voice was low, purposeful but not unpleasant. In fact, grudgingly, Mildred had to admit that Madame Levitte had a curious sort of charm, the same which she recalled having been possessed by the man she herself had been in love with for so many years. 'I do not wish to intrude,' it went on, 'nor do I wish to embarrass the Rayner family. That is why I am so glad to have met someone so *sympathique* who could perhaps help me.'

Madame Levitte stood there in the April sunshine, a tall well-built woman, dressed today in a beige woollen outfit, her coiffure immaculate, her eyes, with their carefully applied mascara, searching and intelligent. Reginald's eyes, Mildred thought. 'You had better come in,' she said.

Mildred led her up to her own flat and then, a little uncharacteristically, came straight to the point.

'What is it you want?'

Madame Levitte replied with equal directness, 'Nothing material, I assure you. I am a rich woman, but a lonely one. My husband died a year ago and, soon afterwards, my adoptive parents. I decided to travel, but first I went to see my natural mother.'

'Your *natural* mother?'

'Yes. Her identity had been kept from me until just before my adoptive mother died. She told me about my origins more or less on her deathbed, thank God. And then, mercifully, I was able to learn so much more from my real mother before she, too, passed on. Tell me, did you not ever think . . . ?'

Miserably, Mildred looked away and then back to her visitor.

Presently, Madame Levitte continued, 'My mother was very beautiful, even at eighty-seven. I could see that. Very quiet, very soft-spoken. She was Egyptian. I found her living the life of a recluse just outside Alexandria. She did not seem to want the usual things others expect from this world.'

'Wasn't it a shock? Your coming to see her?' Mildred seemed to have found her voice at last.

'No, not really. I had given her warning, naturally. I found there was such a serenity about her. I don't know how much this applied when she had been a young girl, when she knew my father. I suspect she may always have had this quality. It could easily have been the one which initially drew them together. I gather he was a loner. Someone who disliked social life.'

'Yes.'

'But I suppose that at some time they must both have been overtaken by the same physical urges which affect the rest of mankind. Hence, after all, my birth.'

'Was she not bothered by that and . . . well, allowing you to be adopted?'

'Yes, very much so, especially at the time, I gathered. It turned her towards a religious life, a life of atonement.'

'How . . . often did Sir Reginald visit her after the adoption?' Mildred felt she had to know. The answer was important to her. Surely this man whom she had idolised wouldn't have simply backed out of all his responsibilities once arrangements for the child had been satisfactorily taken care of.

'Oh, he came to see her right up until the time he died. Although I don't think there was anything physical between them after I was born. I suppose they both suffered acute remorse.'

'And he never attempted to see you?'

'No. How could he? The agreement was that there would be a complete severance of communication. The couple who adopted me were wealthy. He was an Egyptian shipping merchant, his wife was French. They were carefully vetted, of course. It wasn't easy in those days. But they couldn't have been kinder. They gave me a first-class education. After schooling I was sent to Paris. The war was over by then. I stayed on to study art and interior design. Then I met my husband, a French architect.'

'And you never knew who your real parents were?'

'No. Not, as I said, until my adoptive mother was dying. I suppose she thought she ought to tell me then. I was pretty much alone. My husband had died and I never had any children. It was a conscious decision on my part. I had . . . how do you say? . . . a hang-up about being adopted.'

'What did your natural mother tell you when you went to see her?'

'She said that I had been on her conscience all her life, that her love for my father had been something quite apart, out of context. When she became pregnant her family disowned her. They were fairly high up in government circles. My father supported her until she refused any further assistance and took to a life of self-denial, helping those much more in need than herself. She was then cared for by the same organisation to which, in previous years, she had devoted all her own energies.'

'And now? What has made you come here, knowing that Sir Reginald has been dead some time? I don't quite see . . .'

'No, Madame? But are you not in the fortunate position of belonging to a family, maybe two families? My mother told me how you were held in great affection and respect by the Rayners and I dare say you have relatives of your own.'

'I have a brother, yes.'

'Who has children?'

'Yes.'

'Then you are lucky. You have an interest in the younger generation.'

Mildred thought of Rory and remained silent.

'My mother told me a lot about where my father had lived. I felt I had to see this house and, if possible, to find out what had happened to his wife and his other children after his death. My luck was in for, quite by chance, in the hotel where I am staying, I came across a picture of Crane Lodge being advertised for sale in *Country Life*. At least, I thought, I can go and have a good look at it, although I had no idea I would have the pleasure of meeting you.'

'But now that you have?' Mildred surprised herself by her own assertiveness.

'Madame, cannot you understand? The estate agents told me that Lady Rayner was dead, but somewhere I must have a half-brother and a half-sister. I presume they are still alive?'

Mildred coloured. 'You wish to meet them?'

'Yes. More than anything in the world. Would you be prepared to let me have their addresses?'

There was a long silence in the room then. Presently Mildred said, 'You are asking something of me which I am not sure I can give. I think, for reasons which I feel unable to divulge, it might be better if you left well alone.'

'But surely . . . Cannot you give me some idea of these reasons? Then it would be up to me to decide.'

It was, Mildred knew, a perfectly reasonable and logical response. And, after all, even if she tried to prevent such a meeting, this woman before her would no doubt find her information through other means. She was, Mildred suspected, used to getting her own way. She would simply go to the estate agents and ask them the name of the solicitors handling the estate. It would only be a question of time. Bernard and Joanna would be tracked down in the same way as she had just been.

Wearily, Mildred supplied Madame Levitte with the addresses she wanted.

21

'So Crane Lodge is sold at last,' said Felicity, when she came to collect George who, though having missed out on a holiday with his friends, was pleased to think he was due back at school next day and would not have more than twenty-four hours under his mother and stepfather's roof.

'To some city tycoon, I believe,' she went on. 'A good thing. The place needs a complete uplift. It's always seemed to me the most depressing kind of home or, rather, it never really was one, was it?'

Mildred felt annoyed and hurt. It was the only home she had known for most of her life. She knew what Felicity meant for she, too, had often thought the same way about it but, nevertheless, she did not like such sentiments being spelled out in so many words by someone who, after all, was not exactly a home-maker, judging by some of George's unpremeditated remarks.

If only she herself, Mildred thought, could have had a hand in turning Crane Lodge into less of a museum or, indeed, mausoleum. If only she could have persuaded Gloria to spend money on prettier furniture and furnishings. Sometimes Mildred felt that her own apartment was the only bright spot in the whole, dark, unloved and unlovely establishment. She could hardly wait to leave it now, especially as she had just put down a deposit on a small flat not far from Bertie at Strand-on-the-Green, which seemed to be exactly what she wanted. And I shall be close at hand if need be, she could not help thinking, the desire to be of service to others intrinsic to her character.

'Will you be coming to the furniture sale on May 7th?' she enquired of Felicity, as she said goodbye to her and George.

Bernard's wife gave a short laugh. 'I don't think so. There's no point, unless it's to bid up the lots. We've got what we want, even if we have been subjected to the outrageous business of having to pay for it. We shall just have to hope that masses of people turn up on the day and the auctioneers do their stuff. I gather there's going to be a good deal of razzmatazz, a marquee and a refreshment tent and all that. I must say they've done quite well over advertising. So did the estate agents, for that matter, over the house itself. Did you get many viewers?'

'Quite a few.'

'Of course, there are always busybodies who will come and gawp at anything. Bernard had a telephone call from a weird Frenchwoman the other day, saying she'd looked over Crane Lodge as she had a particular interest in it. She said she didn't want to buy the place but she wondered if she could come and talk to him about it. Do you recall seeing her?'

'I think so. What did Bernard say?'

'Well, she caught him on one of his better days. He's fixed up to see her some time. I suppose he might as well. He's got nothing else to occupy him now, has he? Please God, he won't be sloshed, though. It's so embarrassing.'

Mildred waved them goodbye and went back indoors to think. So Madame Levitte was on the trail, was she. She would be sure to contact Joanna soon. Mildred felt she needed to talk to someone about the situation at once and Bertie was the obvious answer. She went over to the telephone and rang him up. After all, the two of them were the same generation, or near enough. Mildred had often sensed that they knew things which, for various reasons, they kept to themselves. Would it not be best, now, to bring them out into the open, at least, so far as they were concerned?

He looked frailer when she drove over to see him that afternoon, but there was no doubt about how pleased he was to see her. She suspected that these days his visitors were few, that he lived more and more in the past and that any contact with someone connected with that past was precious. Rather like Joanna, over the previous eight months she had come to realise Bertie's worth, that he was not the shallow philanderer she had once thought him, that his association with Gloria had not, perhaps, been without justification, especially when she thought about recent developments. Mildred was anxious to lead up to that gently. She did not want to cause any shock. On the other hand, she had a feeling that he might even welcome a heart-to-heart about it all.

After a few initial pleasantries, she said, quietly, 'By the way, I had a visitor the other day. She arrived on the pretext she wanted to view the house.'

'Yes?' He did not seem particularly surprised, but she noticed him watching her carefully.

'She was a foreigner. A Madame Levitte.' Mildred hesitated, wondering whether, after all, she had been right in her decision to unburden herself to him. It was a relief when he said, quite simply, 'Reginald's daughter.'

'Yes. I imagined . . . you knew there was a child.'

He nodded. 'It was one of the reasons why Gloria seemed to need so much more than . . . just an escort. Way back.'

'Was it before . . . Joanna was born?' Mildred was surprised at her own temerity.

Bertie nodded again.

'And you don't think Jo ever guessed that she . . .?'

'Yes, I do. After she grew up. But whatever she suspected, she probably did her best to put it out of her mind. It was easier all round that way. She'd never had a good relationship with Gloria and she wouldn't have wanted anything to make it worse.'

They did not speak again for quite a while. Mildred no longer felt like a one-time employee of the Rayner family. Somehow she and Bertie suddenly seemed to be on the same footing. They had a past in common and particularly the welfare of a younger woman, whom they both loved, very much in mind.

'I've been wondering whether and when to tell her,' Bertie said, at last. 'Obviously I should now. I've held back all these years because of a promise I once made to Gloria, but I feel, now, that other considerations take precedence. I'm the only person who can give Joanna the truth. I would not like others to put ideas into her head or for her to be left guessing.'

Once again, surprised at her own audacity, Mildred said, 'There is . . . no doubt?'

'Oh, no. If you recall, Reginald was pretty incapacitated that summer of 1932.'

He bitterly regretted having made the last remark, fearing that he had hurt her and was relieved when she went on, quite matter-of-factly, 'And Gloria knew about his other liaison by then?'

'Yes. Though not about the child until later. I think her pride was hurt more than anything. It may be difficult for you to believe this but, at heart, Gloria lacked self-confidence. However beautiful, she suffered from insecurity. To the world, she wished to present the image of a much-wanted woman. She wasn't keen to have any more children after Bernard's arrival, but when she found she was pregnant again I think, after the initial shock, she was quite pleased, if you understand. It made it look as if her husband . . .' He did not go on.

Mildred thought how so many things were suddenly slipping into place, even though half a century had gone by and it was hard to digest them. It was as if Crane Lodge, reluctantly, was at last yielding its secrets, giving up the ghost, or ghosts, in its death throes. During these last months, she had not merely been sorting out inanimate objects. She had been sorting out lives.

'Now that Madame Levitte is going to see Bernard,' she said, 'perhaps it would be as well if . . .'

'I saw Joanna at once?'

'Yes. I mean, they are not even half-sisters.'

'Do you think there's a chance she might come up and stay the weekend with me? I've already told her to feel free to use this house at any time, particularly after Crane Lodge is sold.'

'Why don't you ring her up? I know she's been very busy with the shop lately, but she could probably do with a break.'

It had to happen, Mildred said to herself, as she drove away. Madame Levitte was simply the catalyst which had brought it about. Mildred did not feel that she particularly liked her and in many ways regretted her appearance on the scene. But she was serving a purpose. It was no longer possible to feel jealousy of the woman's mother, this saintly departed recluse who had evidently once meant so much to Reginald.

It was all such a long, such a very long time ago.

22

He told her, quite simply, after dinner the following Saturday night and when he had finished Joanna was neither surprised nor shocked, only sad. She had been expecting something of this sort for a long time.

She wondered whether she should make some sort of gesture, get up and kiss him perhaps, when he said, suddenly, 'You deserved better.'

'How do you mean?'

'Well, your upbringing. I'm afraid Gloria was hardly the maternal type, Reginald was always away and I myself trying to keep what people call nowadays "a low profile".'

'I had Mildred.'

'Yes, thank God. You had Mildred.'

Presently she said, 'I suppose I go on calling you Bertie? I don't think I could start on Pa or anything at this stage.'

'No, of course not. By the way, there's something I've often wanted to ask you. I hope you don't mind if I do now. You see, I always hoped that you might have made a second marriage which worked out better than the first. Why didn't you marry Sam?'

She gave a wry smile. 'Money.'

'*Money?*' He was surprised. He knew she was far from the avaricious type.

She told him briefly what had happened, that she had still been looking for a shoulder to lean on, thought she had found one in Sam and then how he had tried to get her to behave in a way which was unacceptable to her.

'My moral daughter,' he remarked, with a smile. 'Nowadays, people take rather a different attitude to all that kind of thing. You and Sam still seem to have remained . . . friends, it seems.'

'Oh, yes. We make out. And I've become a lot more independent.'

'All the same, Jo, I do wish you weren't quite so alone. I'm afraid your half-brother is never going to be much use to you.'

'You mustn't worry. As I said, I'm a person in my own

right at last. It's a nice feeling. You must have found that. I've never thought of you as a leaner.'

'Thank you. Although age and infirmity sometimes mean that one is forced to accept help.'

'Well, you've just acknowledged you have a daughter. Don't you go forgetting it.'

'I'm never likely to. But the last thing I want is for you to feel responsible . . .'

She cut him short. 'Now, none of that.' Quickly, she changed the subject. 'I do wonder how Bernard and Madame Levitte will get on.'

'I think it should be an interesting meeting, to say the least. Doubtless he'll get in touch with you, as she will too.'

'When I shall explain that I am no relation of hers. I wonder how she'll take that.'

'She may be a bit taken aback. But from what I could gather from Mildred she's a woman of the world.'

'But a lonely one. Otherwise she surely wouldn't have bothered to try to look us up, that is, if it really isn't money she's after.'

'Mildred didn't seem to think so. It's hard to say. One never knows about other people. Life is full of surprises.'

'Yes. I'd like to be a fly on the wall when she goes to Hampstead. I suppose I must also see Bernard about what you've just told me.'

'I leave that to you. But I must just ask you. This book Sam's doing. I wouldn't want . . .'

'Don't worry. Remember it's a portrait, not a biography. No mention of this will come into it, although I have to say it's something we've talked about between ourselves.'

'So that the confirmation wasn't exactly unexpected?'

'No.'

She thought he looked tired and suggested he turned in. She could hear Mrs Pardoe calling Felix and locking up. She wondered what it would be like to be old and infirm. He had expressesd the wish that she herself was not so alone, but how much worse it must be for him just passing the time until the end.

Yet wasn't that what everyone was doing when it came

down to it, she thought, as she lay awake in bed that night? She had always felt the word 'pastime' singularly apt, even though it was usually associated with pleasure and recreation. But surely work was also a method of passing the time. Look at all those lonely individuals who threw themselves into feverish efforts of one sort or another as soon as they became widowed or divorced. Wasn't she a case in point with her bookshop? True, she had come to like and depend on the work and involvement, but everyone was on a treadmill little or much, she reflected. It simply depended on how one chose to tread.

She began changing her plans with regard to her own life. Was it really so essential to concentrate quite so much on the shop at the expense of her personal domestic affairs? The cottage at Brimley End might have gone, but why not look for another property, one in which she could take care of Bertie should the necessity arise? The shop had done well the past year. The recent accounts showed that. And whatever happened her income would soon be greatly enhanced by her share from Gloria's estate. She was determined not to see Bertie end his days in some institution. He had mentioned how much he had hated the place to which he had been sent to recuperate after his operation.

She was surprised to be woken early the following morning by Mrs Pardoe, who told her she was wanted urgently on the telephone. A host of reasons flitted through her mind as she flung on a housecoat and went downstairs to answer it: Sam? Mildred? Bernard?

'Joanna?' It was Felicity. 'Thank God I've got hold of you. Mildred said you were spending the weekend with Bertie. Can you come? Now, I mean, this minute.'

'I can,' she replied, sensing that, for once, Felicity hardly seemed to be crying wolf, 'but what's happened? Is Bernard . . . ?'

'Bernard has been taken into custody.'

'*Custody?*'

'Yes. He attacked me. I'm a hell of a sight. I'd been expecting something of this sort might happen for some time. He's been getting more and more aggressive. I've been trying to get hold of his solicitor, but it's the weekend

129

and there's no reply from his home number. Do you think you could try Hugh Cory? He's somewhere Richmond way, isn't he?'

Bertie gave Joanna the telephone number of a car-hire firm. She felt perhaps it was important to get to Hampstead as quickly as possible before taking any further steps. Within an hour, Felicity answered the door to her. She had not exaggerated her appearance. Appalled, Joanna could not believe that such disfigurement had been caused by Bernard. She followed her sister-in-law into the drawing-room.

'Apparently he'll be brought back unless I wish to make a charge,' Felicity said. 'But how can I, Jo? Think of the publicity. It's not as if we're exactly unknown, especially round here. And then there's George, poor kid.'

Joanna was relieved to feel that the child's mother had, at least, remembered him. But if Bernard came home, what was to stop the same thing happening again?

'Did you have a row over anything particular?'

'You must know. It's always the same. Gloria's bloody will. Bernard got beside himself. I wouldn't tell this to anyone but you, but when he's been drinking he gets homicidal feelings towards Mildred and Bertie. I suppose last night he vented them on me.'

23

When, from the drawing-room window, Joanna saw the tall well-dressed woman walking towards Felicity's front door she had, until that moment, completely forgotten about Madame Levitte and her proposed visit to Hampstead. Perturbed, she went into the hall to answer the ring, wondering how she could possibly deal with the situation.

Felicity, with her face still most unsightly, was refusing to see anyone other than Joanna and the daily cleaner, who had been told by her employer that she had had a fall – an explanation which Joanna suspected had not been altogether accepted, especially with the sudden disappearance of Bernard. Thanks to his doctor, he was now resident in a special wing of a hospital in the home counties – one of the most expensive in the country – where he was also being attended by a special nurse. 'Specialling', Felicity told Joanna, was costing an extra hundred pounds a day on top of the already exorbitant fees. 'We shall be *ruined*,' she kept moaning, 'and it's so unfair. None of this would ever have happened if Gloria had made a reasonable will.'

Today's visitor, knowing nothing of the circumstances, at first took Joanna to be Bernard's wife. Doing her best to disabuse her, Joanna ushered Madame Levitte into the drawing-room, where she tried to explain Bernard's and Felicity's absence, without going into too many details.

'Hospital, you say? I am so sorry. I do hope it is nothing serious. Poor Mrs Rayner. She must be suffering from strain, yes?'

Madame Levitte appeared genuinely concerned, if disappointed. Joanna, feeling that the reason just put forward for Felicity's indisposition seemed as good as any, merely nodded and let it pass.

'So you have come to . . . how you say in England . . . hold the fort, yes? How kind. You are close, as brother and sister?' the visitor went on.

Joanna now began to feel distinctly uncomfortable. How

could she explain to this unknown *soignée* Frenchwoman half a century of family history? Give character sketches of Reginald, Gloria, Bernard, Felicity, Mildred and Bertie? Besides, what good would it do? No, Madame Levitte must go back to where she came from, forget about the Rayners who were surely no good to her. Suddenly, Joanna felt angry. She had had quite enough shocks and revelations for the moment. She had already been away from her own home and business far longer than she intended. She wanted nothing more than to get away from Hampstead and return to the west country. She had done what she could, she had got hold of Hugh Cory that fateful Sunday morning, been interviewed by the police, seen Bernard into hospital. Felicity must take over the burden, however distasteful and onerous it was. After all, she was his wife. Joanna was only a half-sister, as she had done her best to let Felicity know, as gently as possible.

With a kind of weary desperation, she said, 'Madame, I believe Miss Treadgold advised you to leave well alone. I can only do the same. Things are not what you might imagine. We are not an exactly united or happy family. There are many problems. If it is company you are after, I do not think you will find it here. Please believe me.'

Madame Levitte frowned. Despite her outwardly pleasant manner, Joanna suspected that she was a determined woman, not used to accepting defeat. 'But surely,' she now persisted, 'are you not interested to know more about your half-sister? I should certainly like to know more about you. Sharing a father, is it not possible we have much in common? And do please call me Armelle.'

Quietly, but with equal firmness, Joanna delivered her *coup de grâce*. 'Madame, you are wrong in this assumption. We are not blood relations in any way. Reginald Rayner was not my father. One might, I suppose, reckon we are stepsisters of a sort, although hardly in the eyes of the church or the law.'

'*Mon Dieu!*' Madame Levitte's poise suddenly seemed to desert her. Her face crumpled. She stared at Joanna, disbelievingly. 'I do not understand.'

'No? Well, I never knew for sure until recently. I would

prefer not to discuss the matter. It is complicated and private. The only thing you and I have in common is that we have a half-brother, Bernard, and he, I am sorry to have to tell you, is an alcoholic.'

'*Mon Dieu*,' Madame Levitte said again, under her breath.

Joanna stood up. Her visitor could do no other than follow suit, although she did so unwillingly, obviously still wishing to prolong the meeting, find out more. As Joanna urged her towards the door, Armelle said, 'I must ask you this. It is something I have wondered so much about. In my father's will, did he not leave some token, some acknowledgement of my mother's or my existence? I do not mean anything material.'

'No, Madame.' Joanna hoped that she could at least be described as being cruel to be kind. 'The only person mentioned in his will was my own mother. It was made at the time of his marriage and never altered.'

'I see. Thank you. I will not trouble you again.'

But I *haven't* been kind, Joanna thought, after she had shown her visitor out. I've been unnecessarily unkind. I could have handled the situation better. After all, the woman had not really been any trouble. She had just materialised at an unfortunate time. She watched Madame Levitte from the window again as she walked out of the front gate and looked up and down the road, presumably for a non-existent taxi. It must have been such a blow to her, finding that Reginald had been capable of cutting her out of his life so consistently for so long. And yet, in a way, had not Bertie done that to a lesser extent, over herself? Both men had felt obliged to deny paternity. Bewildered and saddened, she went up to Felicity's bedroom and explained the identity of the visitor, only to be rewarded by a cryptic, 'Well, thank God she didn't want money. That would have been the last straw.'

When, however, Joanna announced that she would have to leave the next day, her sister-in-law's attitude completely changed. To Joanna's horror, she began to weep. Somehow, a swollen-lipped, black-eyed Felicity, with tears pouring down her face, seemed more difficult to cope with than the brusque acid-tongued character who appeared as if she always knew best.

'Oh, Jo, *must* you? I thought you'd be able to visit Bernard. For obvious reasons, I can't at the moment. And then there's George. Who's going to take him out from school the weekend after next? I'm marooned here, as you must see, until my face is better. And, oh God, it's so . . . *lonely.*'

Joanna turned away. Here, in a single morning, were two very different women who had admitted to loneliness. Armelle Levitte might not have expressed her own predicament as blatantly as Felicity, but there was no mistaking it was there, the root cause of unhappiness in so many people's lives.

Joanna walked over to the window looking out over the garden where she had so recently watched the departing figure of the Frenchwoman. Now, all she could see was a lawn in need of cutting and covered with fallen cherry blossom, drooping daffodils and an overgrown hedge, along which clematis ran riot. It was a pretty enough scene, yet it held a certain air of neglect. She had only caught sight of a jobbing gardener once since she had been obliged to remain at Hampstead. Suddenly, she was reminded of something George had said when he had been staying with her. 'Mummy hates gardening. And housework and cooking, too. I think what she'd really like would be to live in a hotel.' Now that Bernard seemed to have gone from bad to worse, would Felicity be able to manage alone? Might she not go downhill, too? Deteriorate into a self-pitying woman unable to look after herself or her son? It was the son for whom Joanna felt untold sympathy. Children were so vulnerable. She guessed George brought out all her repressed and belated maternal feelings.

'If you like,' she said, 'I'll take the child out from school that weekend.'

'Oh, *would* you, Jo?' Felicity searched for her handkerchief. 'He likes you so much. That would be a great relief. But whatever's going to happen to us long term?' There was a fresh bout of weeping. 'With Bernard as he is . . .'

Joanna felt she had had enough. She swivelled round.

This time her voice was harsh. 'Why ever did you marry him?'

Felicity stopped crying. She began putting on her little-girl-lost act, of which Joanna knew she was capable. 'God knows. Why does anyone marry?' she said, twisting her handkerchief round and round. 'Andrew, George's father, ran out on me. I'm hopeless alone. I'd never done a job. Then Bernard came along. He seemed so confident, jolly even, although it's hard to imagine now. He had all the qualities my ex hadn't, strong and successful, or so I thought. Little did I know. I thought George and I were going to be taken care of. Instead, he turned out to be just as bad as Andrew.'

There was nothing, Joanna noted, about love. 'Does George ever see his father?' she asked.

'No. He pushed off abroad.'

'And doesn't the child ask about him?'

'He used to. Not any more, thank God. How could I keep up the pretence he had a fine Daddy when, in fact, he was a mean weak bastard? Now the wretched child will have had two male let-downs. Just as I have. Damned sensible of you never to have remarried.'

Damned sensible of you never to have remarried. The words kept echoing in Joanna's mind when she was in the train on her way home the following day. Was she as sensible as all that? She had never thought of herself as such. It was simply the way that life had turned out for her and she wasn't grumbling. She tried to think of happily married couples whom she knew and found she could not come up with any. A few older ones, perhaps, had survived the years in double harness tolerably well. For some reason the Jamiesons, her mother's neighbours, came to mind, although she did not really know much about them. Of her own generation, most seemed to be divorced or living apart. Marriage must surely be on the way out. There was no point in it. People made vows to stay together until death did them part, but they no longer meant anything. Clergymen now appeared to be quite willing to re-marry divorcees in church, where they gave skilfully thought-up homilies which carefully side-stepped the issue of broken vows. In a hundred years' time – or less, judging by all the co-habitation that went on and the questioning of Christian doctrines – marriage would be an anachronism.

Yes, but what about the children, asked a still small voice? Joanna found she had no answer to that one, only that she must write to George as soon as she got home about taking him out from school.

24

At first Joanna thought that George might be a little too old for the show. But when they were seated in the front row of a small arts theatre in Bournemouth, Joanna realised, thankfully, she was wrong.

George appeared to be in his element, shooting up his hand each time volunteers were invited to come up on stage by Mr Zoraski, the travelling magician. It had been quite by chance that she had seen the advertisement in a west country newspaper two days before she was due to take the child out and, as the weather was unsettled, it had been a great relief when George had said he had never seen what he called a *professional* magician and did Joanna think that Mr Zoraski would saw a woman in half. When the man more than came up to expectations by actually sawing a woman into quarters, George sat spellbound, unable to talk about anything else, as he tucked into sausage and chips and tomato sauce in the tea-shop afterwards.

Although Sam had offered to accompany them, Joanna had decided she would like to entertain the child alone. She felt she wanted to get to know more about this unfortunate boy, who appeared to have such a hopeless background. The idea of buying herself a larger house, in which she could accommodate Bertie if need be, somehow now seemed to embrace the possibility of sometimes catering for George during the holidays.

'Will you be coming again when I'm next due out?' he asked, as she drove him back to school.

Joanna hesitated. Would his mother be able to do that? Would she *want* to do it, even if her face was presentable? What was it Felicity had said to Joanna on the telephone the previous evening? 'I leave it to you how much you tell or don't tell George. He's pretty quick. He's bound to sense something's wrong. I suppose you'd better just say that his stepfather is ill again so I asked you to deputise for me. Of course, we shan't be able to keep up the story for long.'

'I'm not sure about next time, George,' Joanna answered, pretending to concentrate hard on the road ahead. 'I'll certainly come if Mummy can't.'

'But what about half-term? Will I be going to Hampstead then?'

She noticed he did not say home as most children would have done, yet, like all children, he wished to know exactly what was happening and where he stood. Joanna felt she wanted to scream at both Bernard and Felicity. They had no right to do this to an eleven-year-old boy. Why hadn't they *thought* more, why had they not put his security before their own personal aims? And what despicable aims they seemed to have. At the present moment, Bernard's priority appeared to stretch no further than the desire for the next whisky (unless one counted the more devious, possibly subconscious one, of hoping for the demise of at least two of the beneficiaries); as for Felicity, she presumably craved protection – physical, financial and emotional – against all the harsh realities of life. Deep down, she was worse than a child herself.

When they arrived at the school, George insisted that Joanna came in and saw where he slept. She was glad when he informed her that his friend, Tim, who had so disrupted Christmas Day, no longer slept in the same dormitory, although a large boy by the name of James Frampton stared rather rudely at her and told George he would be late for chapel if he didn't buck up. For one awful moment she thought the child was going to cry when she wished him goodbye, but then a kind of mask came over his small pale face and his whole manner changed. He was suddenly off-hand, as he thanked her perfunctorily for the day and disappeared down a passage. She felt like weeping herself as she made her way back to the car.

When she arrived at Sam's house in time for the meal he had promised to prepare for her, she was grateful for the drink he put into her hand and the fact that he did not at once begin to question her on her day. There were things about Sam which she had begun more and more to appreciate. Of course, they were both older now and, she dared to hope, wiser.

'How's the work going?' she enquired, when they were sitting down to fresh salmon, new potatoes and asparagus, her favourite foods and all presented to perfection.

'Coming along. He was an amazing character, you know, this man who you were brought up to believe was your father. Brave to the point of foolhardiness. I suppose that's why he had such an unfortunate end. Never thought about dying. Always thought there was plenty of time for squaring the past, making wills and so forth, when, of course, there wasn't. Incidentally, Mildred rang.'

'Oh? What did she want?'

'She seems to think there's been some hiccup over the sale of Crane Lodge. The tycoon appears to have reneged before contracts were exchanged. He's leaving the country. I dare say he's a swindler.'

'Oh, *no*.'

'Well, it's happening all the time, isn't it? I mean, house sales falling through. Not swindling, although it certainly seems a bit more prevalent these days. But I shouldn't worry. There are plenty more fish in the sea. And it isn't as if you're in the unhappy position of *having* to sell before being able to buy something else. There'll be no need for Mildred to stick there, once the furniture sale's taken place.'

'No, although I dare say she's relying a lot on the trust being set up and a bit of cash being handed out at last. Incidentally, how did she hear about all this at a weekend?'

'Curiously enough, through your Madame Levitte.'

'*Madame Levitte?*'

'Yes. Apparently, she called at Crane Lodge yesterday evening. Mildred seems to think she's now interested in buying the place herself.'

'Good God. And she said she wouldn't trouble us again.'

'Well, it's not exactly troubling you, is it? I mean, not if she's got the wherewithal at the ready.'

'I just don't like it, that's all. It's, well . . .' Joanna searched about in her mind for a suitable adjective, but all she could come up with was 'inappropriate'.

Sam laughed. 'I don't think that's how I'd describe the

situation. It's not as if you're all that attached to the place, is it? It won't exactly hurt you, surely.'

'Maybe not. But it'll upset Mildred. And Bernard, I should have thought – that is, if he ever comes to his senses.'

'Oh, come off it, Jo. How much do you really care about Bernard nowadays? As for Mildred, I get the impression she's sick and tired of the whole thing. She just wants out, especially now her last illusions must have been horribly shattered by the materialisation of Madame L.'

Joanna remained silent, thinking. She knew that, if she were honest, she cared nothing about Bernard and Felicity, and she suspected Sam was probably right in his assessment of Mildred's state of mind. She supposed if Madame Levitte had the money it could not really hurt any of them if she became the new owner of Crane Lodge. There would be no need to see her or ever go near the place again. One could just forget about it. Or could one? Where was it she had read something about dead hands stretching out from the grave? Could a *house* do that? Reginald's and Gloria's hands still seemed to be stretching out far enough, what with wills and trusts and the sheer amount of *clutter* they had left behind them. Maybe Crane Lodge itself had the same kind of tentacles.

Next morning Joanna telephoned Hugh Cory. He did not enquire how she knew that the sale had fallen through, but merely confirmed that this was the case but the estate agents had received another firm offer which they were following up with all dispatch. There was, as usual, one of the countless letters in the post to all the beneficiaries bringing them up to date with the situation.

She wondered whether to tell him she was aware of the identity of the prospective purchaser or whether, perhaps, he knew. It seemed too delicate a subject to bring up on the telephone. Besides, if he did not know, was there any point in enlightening him? It wasn't any business of his, was it, that Sir Reginald Rayner had a daughter out of wedlock who had suddenly turned up and was creating emotional mayhem amongst the beneficiaries? After all, she hadn't told him about her own parentage. Yet Hugh was so involved with them all now. Somehow, it almost seemed deceitful not to put him fully in the picture, especially after the emergency help he had given on the Sunday after Bernard had beaten up Felicity.

Wearily, she put down the telephone and went into the shop. It was usually fairly empty on Monday mornings, but today several people were browsing round and she could hear a voice at the counter bewailing the fact that the book she had ordered for her husband's birthday had not arrived. As soon as she saw Joanna, Mrs Henstridge rushed across to her.

'I can't understand it, Mrs Lawson. If it doesn't come by tomorrow I shall have to have it sent straight from London. I mean, it's a best-seller, isn't it?'

Joanna tried to remain patient and polite. The woman was one of her regular customers but, for once, the shop and all its demands irritated her. She was unable to forget the new twist of events in her private life.

'I'm afraid that's the trouble, Mrs Henstridge, as I think I mentioned before. I doubt you'll get the book anywhere as it's being reprinted, but I'll make further enquiries and let you know the position later today.'

Unconvinced, Mrs Henstridge departed and Joanna returned to her office. She supposed she could have telephoned the publishers there and then, but there were certain other calls which she suddenly felt must take priority. Usually, she left her personal ones until the cheaper rate in the evening. But this was different. Why had Madame Levitte decided she wanted Crane Lodge? She must have some other motive than loneliness or a wish to gain an entrée into the family of the father she had never seen. She had not struck Joanna as being a particularly sentimental woman, although one could never tell about other people, as Bertie had remarked when she had last seen him. And what was it that judge had said the time Joanna had been obliged to do jury service and there had been a young man, of hitherto impeccable character, who was being tried for whiling away a boring afternoon by taking pot shots at passers-by with an air-gun: 'We shall never know what came over him, the workings of the

141

human mind being incomprehensible.' What had come over Madame Levitte?

Mildred's voice on the other end of the line seemed unusually faint, almost defeated, Joanna thought, when she got through to her and asked where the woman was staying.

'I don't know,' she replied, 'but she seems to want Crane Lodge very much now.'

'But have you any idea why? Something must have made her change her mind. If she's lonely, it's surely far too large a place to live in by herself.'

'I don't think she's going to.' Mildred's voice had begun to be even querulous. 'She said something about retaining just a few rooms for herself as she had other ideas for the rest of the house.'

25

'Another aperitif?'

Joanna shook her head. Things were not going at all as she would have wished.

'Then perhaps we should have lunch?'

Madame Levitte rose. She was wearing a grey chiffon, floating kind of ensemble, there were new highlights in her hair and she seemed very much in command of the situation. A waiter led them to a corner table in the main dining-room of the Ritz. Joanna's own invitation to a less grand establishment had somehow been turned round so that, against her will, she found herself on the receiving end of Armelle Levitte's undoubtedly generous hospitality.

'You seemed surprised,' the latter said, after they were seated and a waiter had taken their orders, 'that I have stepped in and am hoping to buy Crane Lodge.'

'Well, yes. You did not appear to want it the last time we met. Your intentions seem to have taken a rather dramatic turn. Maybe I have no right to ask but I couldn't help wanting to know the reason.'

'There is nothing sinister about it, I assure you,' Armelle replied. 'In fact, quite the reverse. I changed my mind after my visit to your sister-in-law's house.'

Joanna frowned. She felt that Armelle was enjoying keeping her in suspense and she was therefore at a disadvantage. What she had hoped might have been a quiet informal little tête-à-tête, primarily because Joanna was concerned about Mildred's anxiety over the latest development, was becoming a cross-examination in a public and extremely sophisticated place. The ambience of the Ritz unnerved her. She was conscious that her clothes were a give-away. She was simply a small-town country bookseller, no match for this woman who was so very much at home in one of London's smartest hotels. Joanna wished devoutly that she had not initiated the meeting. But the dogged determination which had carried her through previous vicissitudes helped her to persist.

'I can't see what your visit to Hampstead can have to do with buying Crane Lodge.'

'No? Let me explain myself. You know that my mother devoted her life to the welfare of others. Even if she did once lapse from virtue and subsequently had me adopted, she turned into a saint. She *atoned*, as it were. I have not got her qualities. I have, for too long, become used to the good things of life.' Here, Armelle Levitte waved a hand vaguely, as if indicating that such things were all around them. 'Nevertheless, I am lonely and it occurred to me how much the rich as well as the poor suffer in this respect. Your half-brother, and mine, for instance. And his wife. Forgive me, but after that day I met you, I made certain enquiries.'

Joanna wondered whom she had approached. Hugh Cory? A private detective?

'It wasn't easy,' Armelle went on, in an annoyingly mysterious way. 'People here are very discreet, but I learned enough. It seemed to me that what with my not inconsiderable assets, I might provide a *service*, one for which others would pay. I am not as philanthropic as my late mother. But I intend to turn Crane Lodge into a rest home. I thought I would change the name. The Rayner Rest Home sounds rather good, don't you think? And possibly, later on, if another suitable house comes up for sale in the district, I might acquire that for those who need, well, a little more than just a rest.'

The waiter brought a bottle of Chablis, opened it and poured out a little for Armelle to taste. She took a sip and indicated that he should fill Joanna's glass.

'You would need permission from the authorities for all that kind of thing.' Joanna tried to remain unsurprised and matter-of-fact.

'Of course. I have anticipated that. I have already been to see them. My late husband was a very well-known architect who was responsible for the renovation of two famous hospitals in Paris after the war. And I am not without credentials myself. I think I mentioned that I studied interior decorating as well as art in my youth. I believe I could turn Crane Lodge into an extremely pleasant but practical establishment, once much of its existing structure was gutted. I should naturally employ expert assistance. But just think, it has the great asset of being close to Richmond Park and, properly landscaped, the grounds would be perfect for those in need of temporary retreat from the stresses and strains of daily life. Our half-brother and his wife, as I've already said.'

'Oh.' It was difficult to appreciate that Bernard was both Armelle's and her half-brother, that he and she had had the same mother and that Armelle and he had had the same father. Joanna drank some wine. She felt in need of it. She had a sudden mental picture of all them resident under Armelle's roof and at her mercy: Bertie, Mildred, Bernard and Felicity, even herself and Sam. Why, the woman was insatiable. There was no stopping her. If her ancient mother had been alive she would probably have brought her over from Egypt to end her days at Crane Lodge.

'I wondered whether to contact you again about this,' Armelle continued, equably, 'but I felt you were hostile towards me. I'm glad you got in touch. I hope we can now be friends.'

Joanna drank some more wine and a waiter filled up her glass. Another placed an avacado mousse in front of her. She looked at it with distaste. She had no appetite and no wish to be friends with this woman who had just come into her life, although she could not quite understand why. Madame Levitte had not personally done her any harm. In fact, she had come to the rescue by stepping in to buy Crane Lodge after the first deal had, so unexpectedly and unfortunately, fallen through. Besides, it was not Armelle's fault that Reginald Rayner and some engimatic foreigner had brought her into existence. If she wanted to turn the old family home into a much more useful and sociable place than it had ever been in the past, then perhaps they should all simply wish her luck and let her get on with it. Live and let live. Joanna felt she should have let well alone. After all, that was what both she and Mildred had recommended when Armelle Levitte had wanted to know more about *them*. In her own way, Joanna realised that she was being just as obstructive and defeatist. Yet something propelled her to ask further questions.

'Will you be going to the furniture sale?'

'I've given it a lot of thought. Obviously, the furniture I shall require for a rest home will be very different from most of that which is at present in the house. Possibly I might bid for a few practical items: bookcases, garden seats and that sort of thing. But if, as I anticipate, there are to be major structural alterations, then I really feel it would be best to furnish from scratch. I intend . . . how shall I put it? . . . to *lighten* Crane Lodge. Pale colours, white paint, floral prints, flowers. Forgive me, but I think perhaps it is a house where there has not been enough of that.'

When Joanna did not answer, Armelle went on, swiftly changing the subject, 'Tell me about Mildred. She interests me.'

'Mildred? She is one of the chief, if not *the* chief reasons I wanted to see you again. Crane Lodge has been her *life*. She has had a wretched time clearing it up. I don't think she would at all mind it being turned into a rest home, if it were not for . . .'

'For the identity of the person who intends to put that into practice?'

'Yes, but how did you know?'

'My dear Joanna. I may call you that, mayn't I? I do wish you'd bring yourself to call me Armelle. I am not a fool. She adored my father, didn't she?'

There is not much, Joanna thought, which gets past you. Not for the first time did she realise what an astute woman she was up against.

'You know, I suppose, that she will be living in the district?'

'Yes, so she tells me. And I have told her that she must feel free to visit her old home whenever she feels like it. I can assure you that such an invitation extends to you all. I understand there is a Mr Fane . . .' For the first time, Armelle Levitte hesitated slightly, 'who is also a beneficiary under the terms of the late Lady Rayner's will. It would be so nice to meet you all, especially my relative, Bernard. I gather he is still in hospital.'

'Yes.' But *how* did you gather, Joanna wondered. Do you have spies out? Belong to MI5? I wouldn't put anything past you. You *must* have been in touch with Hugh Cory, even though I know he would have been the soul of discretion. But there's no doubt that you've insinuated yourself into our lives and today I've assisted you, damn it. I know that whenever I do receive any money from that blessed trust I shall feel that you are personally handing it out. It's almost as if, in buying Crane Lodge, you're buying us all. I can't really believe you're as lonely as you've made out. You're too forceful a character.

'Will you be spending much time at Crane Lodge?' Joanna asked, returning to the attack.

Armelle Levitte looked surprised. 'Why yes, particularly at the beginning, *naturally*.' Joanna noted how singularly fond her hostess seemed of that adjective, as she listened to her continuing, 'Of course I shall probably have to find some nearby accommodation as things progress. There will be so much supervision needed. If one is not on the spot things are apt not to get done or, if they are done, then not as one would have wished. I dare say you find that in your bookshop. And I shall have to think about staff. A qualified matron, a housekeeper. If Mildred had been younger, she would have been ideal for the latter role.'

Joanna could feel her temper rising. 'Mildred,' she said, with an asperity which surprised her, 'is not a housekeeper.'

'No? I'm sorry, but once upon a time, maybe.'

'Mildred,' replied Joanna, slowly, 'is a friend of the family. She has an equal share in my late mother's estate and has done more than anyone else towards preserving it.'

Armelle Levitte inclined her head. Then she said, 'Once again, you must forgive me. I think my only answer to that can be, how do you say in your country . . . point taken?'

26

None of them had meant to go and yet, on the first day of the sale, there they all were, drawn by some kind of mutual empathy and curiosity, picnicking in the empty room once occupied by the troublesome Rory and then an ailing George. Felicity had even been able to bring a subdued Bernard as well as her son, who happened to be home for half-term that week. There was a pooling of sandwiches, sausage rolls, fruit, coffee and Coca Cola – no alcohol by tacit agreement, in deference to the reformed character in their midst.

The doctor who had been treating Bernard in the latest hospital had, by sheer ruthlessness, somehow got through to him that he had two choices: stop drinking altogether or be dead within six months, probably earlier. Hitherto, the thought of death in connection with himself was something from which Bernard had invariably shied away. Now, he seemed to have become aware of the fact that he would more than likely be the first beneficiary to die, that it was most unlikely he would inherit the capital and that, because of his appalling attack on his wife – about which he seemed genuinely sorry – he owed it to her to make a supreme effort to mend his ways. Felicity had, moreover, made it quite clear that one more lapse and she would sue for divorce – however terrified she felt about being on her own again – and, after his recent behaviour, Bernard was well aware that it would be a divorce for which he would be made to pay, heavily.

He had therefore given a solemn promise that if he were allowed home he would visit a colleague of the said doctor on a daily basis for an indefinite period. This man lived, conveniently, in Hampstead, and had agreed to see Bernard at eight thirty each morning except weekends, when he was asked to keep in touch by telephone. Such an arrangement was humiliating, expensive – although not as expensive as hospitalisation – and, in a rare flash of his old humour, Bernard had referred to Dr Freeman as 'my probation officer'. So far, to Felicity's amazement and relief, the treatment appeared to be working.

Bernard had also begun to take an interest in his late mother's estate again, particularly the sale of the house to his half-sister. Madame Levitte had made a second visit to Hampstead and the meeting had gone off surprisingly well. Bernard had even joked that he would probably end his days where they had begun and had, in fact, become quite intrigued by Armelle, so much so that Felicity wondered whether, from having an alcoholic on her hands, she now had a case of incipient incest. But then she dismissed the idea as ridiculous. Whatever the present situation, it was altogether preferable to that which had been taking place for some considerable time.

The enormous attendance at the sale surprised everyone. The bidding was brisk and it seemed that although Gloria's possessions *in situ* had never created a particularly pleasing impression, nevertheless, individually, they had a unique quality which dealers and the public were quick to appreciate.

George had set himself up as a kind of runner, continually going off into the marquee and then breathlessly rushing back to the house with the news that some lot or other had been knocked down for 'a cool thou', an expression he had recently picked up at school.

Once or twice, Bernard and Felicity had made discreet little sorties into the tent themselves, conversing with a few people whom they recognised, particularly Armelle Levitte who, although buying little, was much in evidence, dressed somewhat flamboyantly in fuchsia-coloured silk. But for various reasons, the others stayed where they were. Bertie was, in any case, not up to facing the heat and the crowds, while all were conscious that it hardly seemed appropriate to appear overtly interested in the prices being fetched. Mildred, actually, appeared to have scarcely any interest in the fact that with every knock of the hammer she was appreciably richer, for the finality of it all had suddenly begun to hit her and she was wondering how soon she could suggest to Bertie that she would drive him back to Strand-on-the-Green, after which she would be able to slip away to her own little home, where there was still so much to do.

Towards the middle of the afternoon, Joanna also felt that she and Sam should be thinking about getting back to the west country. For once, it had been a pleasant forgathering of the beneficiaries, but now it was time to go their separate ways. She had been glad to see Bernard looking and behaving so much better, Felicity's face restored to normal, George happier and Bertie and Mildred supporting each other in such a tender and friendly fashion. Most of the best items in the sale had been sold and she knew that the following day it would merely be second-class stuff. She was on the point of packing up their picnic things when George came rushing into the room, his eyes alight with excitement.

'There's been a scrittor sold for five thou,' he burst out.

'A scrittor?' Felicity frowned and studied her catalogue. 'Oh, you mean an escritoire, darling.'

'Good God. The little desk in Gloria's sitting-room. It can't possibly have fetched that.' Bernard stared at his stepson in disbelief, before saying to his wife, 'Why on earth didn't we earmark it?'

'You must remember. You said you didn't like it. You'd sooner have the second bureau bookcase.' Felicity turned to her son again. 'Do you know who happened to buy it, George?'

'Not his name,' the boy replied, 'but I saw what he looked like. I watched him bidding. He was that funny old chap you spoke to earlier on. The one with the white hair and side whiskers.'

'Oh, Mr Jamieson. Fancy that. I'd no idea he was a connoisseur of antiques and would pay such a price.'

In the ensuing buzz of conversation, Mildred remained silent. She thought, as she often had, about the visit the Jamiesons paid Gloria shortly before her death and then of her own visit to them on that fateful night earlier in the year. She, too, was surprised that John Jamieson had seen fit to pay so much for the escritoire, although he was obviously a man of considerable wealth. She had never forgotten how he and his wife seemed to assume that everyone was on the same level as themselves and how they had expected her to remain at Crane Lodge. But, being

Mildred, the financial aspect of George's latest revelation meant far less to her than the purely emotional one. Rather as if she were personally parting with a beloved pet, she was glad to feel that at least one item from Crane Lodge would be going to a good home nearby, where it would be properly appreciated and where she might occasionally even see it again. Like Joanna, she too felt it was now time to depart. Quietly, she began packing up the picnic basket which she had brought for Bertie and herself.

After goodbyes all round, she shepherded him out of the back door and into her waiting car – which everyone had insisted she should keep, along with the rather more doubtful asset, Jason – and took one last look at Crane Lodge. Then she quickly got into the driving-seat and started up the engine. She did not look back. Nor did she think she would come there again, however kind and pressing Madame Levitte had been in asking her to visit the place whenever she so wished. Somehow, the images of all those rooms she had known for over half a century, however uncomfortable and unattractive they might have been, were so indelibly etched on her memory that she felt it would be distressing to see them turned upside down and inside out. Of course, if and when infirmity caught up with her, she was well aware she might have to go into residential care but, even with her improved circumstances, she doubted she would be able to afford the kind of fees Madame Levitte would charge. For the moment, she would try not to think about it. She was still fit and able, thank God, even if she *was* now feeling just a little jaded by the events of the day.

Something of the same thoughts were going through Bertie's mind as she drove him slowly back to Strand-on-the-Green. He had naturally never had the same attachment to Crane Lodge as Mildred, for his own home meant much to him and he hoped fervently he could remain in it to the end of his days. On the other hand, he had no doubt that Armelle would make a good job of the conversion she was contemplating. The Rayner Rest Home would surely be extremely comfortable and well run, if expensive. But what was that? Unlike Mildred, he would have the

wherewithal. With his present assets and selling, if un-
avoidable, his own home, together with the income from
the trust – which would surely not be long in coming
through now – he would have more than enough to see
him out. That sale today had been an eye-opener, even if
there would unquestionably be a bit more tax to pay.

Joanna remarked on just the same thing once she was
being driven home by a somewhat preoccupied Sam. He
agreed that he would never have imagined such high
prices, that the auctioneers were to be congratulated and
he hoped Bernard was duly satisfied. When they were
nearly home he suggested stopping for an early dinner at
a road-house they occasionally visited. To Joanna, it
seemed the most pleasant way of ending what had been
an altogether satisfactory day. It was not until they were
sitting out in the garden having coffee after the meal that
her feeling of contentment was abruptly ended.

Without any warning, Sam suddenly leaned across the
wooden table between them and said, 'Jo, how would you
feel now about getting married after all?'

27

Joanna was depressed, more depressed than she had been for a long time. At least Sam could have *waited*, she felt, a little longer. Presumably, the fantastic result of the sale had so bowled him over that he had not been able to refrain from making this new and totally unexpected proposal.

Now, far from looking forward to her increased wealth and, Joanna was forced to admit, in all probability one day much greater wealth, it was spoiling a relationship which meant, despite its one-time difficulties, much to her. Was it a male prerogative, she wondered, this obsession with money? Certainly Bernard and Sam had it. So had her former husband, and even little George had appeared excited over all those 'cool thous' at the sale; although Bertie, bless him, seemed able to remain fairly detached on the subject.

Of course, when she came to think more about it, females were far from immune from the disease. What about the proverbial gold-digger? Or even women simply seeking security in marriage? Take Felicity, for example; and Joanna knew that she herself was by no means averse to whatever was coming her way. Only Mildred seemed capable of ignoring materialism. She was a person without greed or guile. It must be nice, Joanna felt, to have no acquisitive streak in one's make-up at all.

Joanna had not seen Sam for a week now. She had made it quite clear that his proposal was unwelcome, but she was not quite sure what her next move should be. He had not yet finished the portrait and there was still the disposal of Reginald's archive to see about after that. Obviously some kind of contact would have to be maintained.

Moreover, Joanna could not quite conceive of life without Sam. Something, not just occasional sex, still made him necessary to her. She might have fancied she was an independent woman but, when it actually came to the point, she realised now that she was far from that. Then, quickly following in its footsteps there came another thought: would it be such a bad thing after all if she and Sam made a permanent commitment to one another, joined forces and bought some rather nice property, settled down and started to do what she felt Gloria had never done: grow old gracefully? That would certainly mean marriage. However emancipated the times, she did not think they could get away with living together in the little west country community which already, she knew, had reservations about them. That customer who had made such a fuss about her husband's birthday present was but a case in point. Although Joanna had managed to procure for her one of the very first copies of the second printing, the woman never came into the shop now and it was rumoured that it was because she felt Mrs Lawson was allowing her complicated private life to interfere with the running of her business. Even little George had shown some embarrassment about Sam and Joanna's relationship, so that if the child, or Bertie for that matter, ever came to spend much time with them – and she did not think that Sam would object to this – it would be better, surely, to bow to convention. It didn't really matter, did it, if she was the one with the money?

The immediate problem was: how to get back on better terms with Sam? He could be amazingly stubborn when he felt like it.

Happily, the solution was taken out of her hands when he suddenly turned up one evening, just as he had done once before. He had a bottle of champagne and an apology. He said he was sorry and realised how much he had upset her, but that his proposal had not been as calculated as she had imagined. It had been primarily instigated by a conversation he had had with Bertie when they found themselves alone together for a while at the sale. Bertie had voiced the same fears about which Joanna had recently, if reluctantly, become aware: that she was not nearly the hard-headed business woman she made herself out to be and Bertie apparently wished that she had some sort of safer anchorage.

'Without putting it in so many words,' Sam explained, 'the old boy would obviously like to see you settled before he passes on. And I honestly don't think he takes quite such a poor view of me as you do.'

Mollified, and comforted by tenderness and champagne, Joanna had woken up the next morning to find herself an engaged woman. Quite apart from anything else, she felt, the Crane Lodge sale had sorted out at least one long-standing emotional question mark.

Felicity also had been pleased to think that it had marked an achievement in Bernard's rehabilitation. The financial result had, of course, helped; but whereas he still might have remained rude or off-hand towards the other beneficiaries, he had behaved a little more like the man she had married. Some of the old confidence and sociability had returned. While Felicity was conscious that Bernard wanted to present himself in as good a light as possible whenever his half-sister was around, there was little doubt in her mind that Dr Freeman had a lot to do with it. She wondered what would happen to her husband without his regular early morning 'work-outs', as she thought of them. Hitherto, Felicity had been sceptical about such treatment. Now, she was not so sure. She did not suppose that Bernard would ever go back to the city but, with judicious handling of his share of the income from the trust, maybe they could get along. Apparently Hugh Cory had organised a highly successful sale of her mother-in-law's jewellery, even if it was quite preposterous that it had not been willed to her.

Both Bertie and Mildred, too, experienced a great sense of relief that something which had been hanging over them all for so long was all but at an end. Mildred, particularly, with so much to do in her new home, wisely put all thought of Crane Lodge out of her mind. She made lists, took measurements, shopped, ran up curtains on her sewing-machine and went about her days in that methodical, seemingly unhurried fashion of hers which invariably produced the required results in an astonishingly short time. After a few weeks, she even began to think about entertaining in a quiet way: Bertie and the Jamiesons, for instance. She had always regretted that she had never got around to returning the latters' kind hospitality while she was still at Crane Lodge, and had allowed the advent and subsequent hasty departure of Rory, followed by the arrival on the scene of George and Madame Levitte, together with the increasing awareness of Bernard's trouble, to preclude it.

Thinking about Rory made Mildred wonder whether she would ask Arnold and Rosie down to stay with her, as soon as the spare room was ready. There had been a coolness after she had written about Rory's sudden departure and how she felt that it was probably all for the best, her nephew's life-style, as she put it, not being compatible with her own. Arnold had demanded to know exactly what had gone wrong, but Mildred suspected that Rosie knew all too well and was embarrassed. There had been no mention of the boy in their subsequent infrequent letters.

Another person who had greatly welcomed the fact that the sale was over was Hugh Cory. He and his partner were already getting to work on the trust, with the help of a firm of top financial advisers. Contracts for the sale of the house had gone through without a hitch. The winding up of the Rayner estate was, thank the Lord, in sight. There was Reginald's archive, of course, to deal with once Sam Foster had no further use for it, but Hugh did not envisage too many problems there. Doubtless, there would have to be provisos about nothing being published without permission from the executors and Sam's own book would have to be vetted for libel or breach of confidentiality, but as far as Hugh was concerned, he was fairly confident that Sam Foster knew what he was about. He had just heard that he and Joanna were getting married quite soon and this seemed excellent news.

Hugh's wife had also profited from the sale, albeit in a small way. Unbeknownst to anyone – except her husband – she had quietly driven over to Crane Lodge, first to view and then to attend each day's sale, on the second of which she had bought a few items. These were of no intrinsic value but, in her opinion, well worth the money as they were just what she wanted: a quantity of old flower-pots, some kitchen utensils and a fish tank, her youngest son having become passionately keen on all forms of aquatic life. But perhaps what was most important to her was finding that she had the courage to bid with the best of them. True, there had been little competition for the lots she had acquired, but she had conquered her fears, raised her catalogue exactly as she had seen the smartly dressed foreign lady do on the first day, a lady who she had ascertained was called Madame Levitte and who 'walked about the place as if she owned it', Hugh's wife had remarked to him afterwards.

'Which she actually does,' he had replied. But being the good lawyer he was, he did not divulge any further information about Armelle Levitte, even when she asked for it.

28

'She does get a move on. I will say that for her,' Bertie remarked, while giving Mildred tea after she had taken him for a drive.

'Yes. At this rate, she could be ready for her first customers by Christmas.'

They hadn't, of course, meant to go anywhere near Crane Lodge, just as none of them had meant to go anywhere near the sale. But it was odd how the house seemed to draw them back to it. Richmond Park was so lovely at this time of the year and what was simpler and more pleasant than for Bertie and Mildred to make their way slowly across it, pausing by the Isabella Plantation and then going on to do a detour round some of their old haunts.

Today, though screened from view by chestnut and maple trees in full leaf, Crane Lodge was obviously a place of great activity. The drive along which Mildred had walked with such trepidation that winter's night six months ago was more like a busy road, builders' vans and lorries going up and down, even a despatch rider on a motorcycle roaring away at one point, presumably having delivered some vital communication to whomsoever was in charge.

Suddenly Bertie said, shyly, as he passed Mildred a plate of Mrs Pardoe's fairy cakes, 'I've actually put my name down, you know.'

'*Have* you, now?' She was not altogether surprised. In fact, when she came to think about it, it was probably the most sensible thing he could have done.

'Well, Mrs Pardoe's arthritis has been troubling her much more lately and I felt, what with one thing and another, I might one day have to give up at Strand-on-the-Green, much as it will be a wrench. But even if I never have to do so, it's as well for my name to be on a list at the Rayner Rest Home. Then, every time a vacancy comes up, one's case can be reviewed. I can't think of a better place. It's in my area. I'm sure it will be well run and not institutionalised. I've opted for a ground floor although, naturally, Armelle is putting in lifts.'

'*Lifts?*' Mildred tried to imagine it. Crane Lodge with lifts. It was unbelievable. She thought of all those years when she had gone up and down the stairs, carrying children, carrying trays, helping an inebriated Gloria back to her bedroom at night and, latterly, lugging memorabilia and sacks of rubbish from one storey to another. The idea of possibly sitting back in comfort in the same house, while others actually waited on *her*, made Mildred feel quite giddy and lighthearted – almost guilty, in fact. It was like being tempted by the devil himself.

As if reading her mind, Bertie went on, 'Have you ever thought of doing the same? I mean, let's hope it won't ever be necessary but, as I said, there's no harm done in putting your name down for a room. It doesn't commit you. And from the letter we've all just had from Hugh Cory, it seems we can each expect more income than we've bargained for.'

'No. Yes. I mean, I suppose it's a thought.' Since her unfortunate experience over Rory, Mildred knew that she was not quite so keen about passing on her own estate to the younger generation and had, in fact, altered her will. She supposed it might be possible, after all, for her to afford perhaps one of the smaller rooms in the Rayner Rest Home. 'How did you contact Armelle?' she asked Bertie. 'Did you write direct to Crane Lodge?'

'Yes, and I got a charming letter back. Apparently, she's taken a flat above that excellent new restaurant where Jo and Sam once gave us lunch. Trust her to fall on her feet. She went there for a meal and heard that the proprietor and his wife had done up their top floor for their son, who is returning from America next year to help them with the business. Until then, they said they were quite willing to let it to Armelle. I imagine she found sleeping at Crane Lodge, with all the work in progress, too uncomfortable, but still wanted to be as on the spot as possible. She's even got as far as planning some brochure, although of course she won't be able to have any photographs taken yet awhile.'

'Have you told Joanna all this?'

'No. But I shall, as soon as she's back from her honeymoon. I wanted my decision to be a *fait accompli*, so to speak. I believe she and Sam are thinking of buying some larger property and I'm afraid it's with me in mind. Dear girl that she is, I really do want to remain as independent as I can. Besides, she's newly wed. Much better for her and Sam to be by themselves.'

Bertie's latest disclosure gave Mildred a lot to think about as she drove back to her own home that evening. How sensible and selfless he was, she thought. As one got older it was always wise to make one's own arrangements as far as possible and let one's views be known. It was almost as important as making a will, this business of deciding how to spend one's declining years before one actually passed on. Neither Gloria nor Reginald ever seemed to have given the matter a thought although, fortunately for them, in both cases it was taken out of their hands: Reginald's by sudden death, Gloria's by having Mildred to attend to her every whim and that of her equally spoiled and tiresome little dog.

She tried hard not to think about it, but Mildred had been relieved when Jason, shortly after leaving Crane Lodge, had suffered a fatal heart attack. Already old and enfeebled and far from being any kind of companion, he had never settled in his new abode, somehow making this very plain by his treatment of her new carpets and general miserable behaviour. After his death, for the first time in her entire adult life, she felt free.

Whatever would have happened, she sometimes wondered, had she herself predeceased her employer? Bernard would hardly have been any use and she couldn't see Joanna, nice as she was and obviously willing to care for Bertie, coping with her mother. Presumably Gloria would have had to go into some kind of private establishment – one which took dogs? – where she would have made a perfect nuisance of herself. A vision of her somehow installed in her former home, being subjected to supervision by Armelle Levitte or her staff rose, with all its bizarre possibilities, unbidden, to Mildred's mind.

Bertie had referred to the larger income they could all now expect and Mildred tried to imagine what this would amount to. There was, of course, still Sam's book – which she understood was finished – to be counted upon, as well as the disposal of Reginald's archive. Mildred did so hope that the latter might be donated and not sold. It somehow did not seem right to be acquiring money for that. But she supposed that Hugh Cory, as the new executor, would probably insist on adhering strictly to the letter of the law and would therefore be bound to try to obtain as much as he could for it on behalf of all the beneficiaries, especially as this was what Bernard would endorse.

How complicated everything was, she thought. How much easier it must have been for someone like Armelle Levitte's mother, who had apparently renounced the world, the flesh and the devil. She must have ended up infinitely rich in the non-material things of life, especially memories, that is, memories of Reginald, for surely, with her temperament, it must have been agony letting her baby be adopted, so much so that it had turned her life into one of atonement. Obviously it hadn't affected Reginald in the same way. Mildred had to admit to herself that her own memory of him had taken a bit of a battering recently. She supposed she had always seen him through rose-coloured spectacles, never allowing for his selfish streak, the desire to go his own way, do his own thing. It would seem that Bernard had inherited a double dose of those traits from both his parents and she could certainly see, or thought she could see, some of them coming out in Armelle. She knew what she wanted, all right, but her aims were at least geared to something far more commendable than her half-brother's. Thank God dear Joanna had turned out to be so like her father. She hoped the girl, as she would never be able to stop thinking of her, was happy now touring somewhere in France with Sam.

Mildred was distressed when Felicity telephoned, later that evening, demanding to know whether she had any idea where Joanna was as she wished to contact her urgently. Bernard, apparently, was not well.

'Is it serious?' Mildred enquired.

'It could be. Very.' Felicity became enigmatic. Mildred could only assume that Bernard had been at the bottle again although, even so, it seemed no reason for spoiling Joanna's honeymoon. There was an uncomfortable pause until Felicity suddenly burst out, her voice devoid of all its recent pleasantness at the sale, 'It's not the old trouble, if that's what you're thinking, although it could be a by-product of it, I suppose. He tripped earlier today and it's my belief he's had a slight stroke.'

'*Stroke?* But what did the doctor say?'

'Nothing much. Silly old fool. By the time he arrived, Bernard was in a deck-chair having his tea in the garden and seemed to have forgotten all about it.'

'But surely, then, there's no need to worry Joanna.'

'I think there is. They've been away over a fortnight. Plenty long enough. And I happen to know Bernard wants to get her agreement to something.'

'But surely it can wait until the end of the week.'

'Not if it *is* a stroke. Besides, Bernard's become so forgetful these days. Sometimes I wonder if he isn't a candidate for that mental disease I can never remember the name of. Mildred, you *must* have a few numbers. I can't believe Joanna would go away without leaving some means of contact. Perhaps she's left her whereabouts with Bertie. She's so potty about him these days. She ought at least to realise her half-brother's far from well and needs a lot of care and attention. She seems to have no idea what I have to put up with.'

Mildred felt trapped. All her common sense told her to withhold details of the itinerary Joanna had given her in case of emergency. She was about to remonstrate with Felicity once more, when an abrupt voice on the other end of the line said, 'O.K. If you're not going to co-operate, I'll ring Bertie or maybe get on to Hugh Cory in the morning.'

With misgiving, Mildred gave Felicity the name of a pension in the Alpes Maritimes, where Joanna and Sam were hoping to stay the following night. She waited while Felicity wrote down the telephone number. Then she heard her say, in the same curt manner, 'Thanks. What wouldn't I give for a holiday myself. Some people get all the luck.'

29

Joanna and Sam were sitting on the terrace of the Villa Marriot, watching the sun going down over the Gorbio valley. Joanna was wondering whether she might give Mildred or Bertie a ring just to see how they were, when the Patron came to say, somewhat excitedly, that there was a call for her from 'Angleterre'. Alarmed, she hurried to answer it.

'Hullo?'

'Joanna?' Felicity's voice seemed to rasp across the continent. 'It's about Bernard.' Even as she knew this was, or appeared to be, an SOS call, Joanna had a feeling that Felicity's concern was more for herself than her husband.

'What about him? What's happened?' she enquired, quickly.

'He's had a stroke.' This time there was no equivocation, no 'I think' about the situation, as there had been with Mildred. 'And he needs to see you,' she went on.

'To see me? Is he very ill? Is it urgent? What does the doctor say?'

There was a fractional hesitation. 'The doctor is keeping him under supervision, naturally. Bernard has been a very sick man for a long time, Joanna. You must know that. He's had a fall and is very shaken up and, of course, his weight is against him these days. There was something he wished to talk to you about before you went off and got married in such a clandestine fashion, if I might say so, and then hopped it abroad.'

'But what's it about? Can I speak to him now?'

'No. Not at the moment. He's sitting in the garden. He doesn't know that I've rung you. He was going to wait until your return. Out of the goodness of his heart,' Felicity added, and the phrase, somehow so incongruous when applied to Bernard, almost made Joanna smile. It was impossible to believe he was as bad as his wife was making out, particularly if he was well enough to be outside.

'We're coming home Saturday night,' Joanna said, 'crossing from Cherbourg to Portsmouth.'

'Can't you make it sooner and come Calais/Dover and call here? You could stay the night if you like, although I suppose you'd rather go to Mildred or Bertie.'

'I don't know,' Joanna replied, doubtfully. 'I'll have to see. We had been intending to spend forty-eight hours at the George V in Paris. I'll ring you as soon as we get there.'

'My God. The George V. You are living it up, aren't you?' Then, using exactly the same words as she had used to Mildred, Felicity continued, 'Some people have all the luck.'

Sam was inclined to be even more sceptical about Felicity's news than Joanna, when she came back to join him on the terrace. 'If she didn't even tell Bernard she was ringing,' he said, 'there's something that doesn't add up. Do you think he really had a stroke or just tripped, as anyone might have done?'

'Heaven knows. But, all the same, it's strange. I suppose we could cancel our berths from Cherbourg and cross from Boulogne or Calais, couldn't we? See what it's all about. I'll go and put through that call to Mildred I was thinking of making anyway. Felicity must have got our whereabouts from her and she might be able to throw a bit more light on everything. I dare say she'd be pleased to put us up. I don't want to worry Bertie, now Mrs Pardoe isn't so good.'

Mildred was, indeed, delighted at the thought of having Sam and Joanna to stay for the Saturday night, although she was unable to account for Felicity's actions, other than to confirm that they appeared to be entirely her own and that Bernard was by no means incapacitated and had, in fact, brushed aside the incident of his fall. She refrained from mentioning Felicity's wild reference to Alzheimer's disease.

Although she did her best not to let it, her sister-in-law's call completely clouded the last few days of Joanna's honeymoon. Up until now it had been a carefree, almost idyllic time. She and Sam had driven slowly, avoiding the main roads as far as possible, stopping at out-of-the-way pensions, enjoying the French food and wine and the conversation – they were both good linguists – of the local inhabitants. Any smart hotel they gave a wide berth, the only concession to this being a couple of nights at the George V on the way home. By more or less unspoken mutual agreement, neither made any reference to all the complications and revelations of the past year. There had not been a single dissension between them.

Now, however, all that changed. Sam, against his will but on Joanna's insistence, started, with difficulty, to cancel their previous travel arrangements. Paris, when they arrived, was sweltering. And, on their last evening, Joanna was suffering from some kind of tummy bug which forced her to remain in their bedroom while he dined alone. Some of the happiest few weeks of her life came abruptly to a premature end.

It was a more gruelling drive to Calais than Cherbourg, and they set out early on the Saturday morning. Sam was taciturn, Joanna still feeling wretched, both mentally and physically. She had often sensed that Bernard wanted to talk to her alone about something he had on his mind and she had a shrewd idea what it might be, but she had no intention of discussing this with Sam until, suddenly, just before they reached the outskirts of Amiens, he said, to her amazement, 'I suppose your precious half-brother wants to do a deal with you.'

'A deal?' She affected complete surprise and ignorance.

'Yes. Well, it's sticking out a mile, isn't it? He couldn't stomach the idea of Mildred and Bertie getting their hands on any capital. I reckon he's been hoping that at least Bertie would have passed on by now. As he hasn't and Mildred appears to be still going strong, I expect he's hoping to get you to enter into some agreement that once they have departed, you and he can break the trust and have outright shares. The fact that you've now acquired a husband and Bernard himself is not too good a risk makes it all seem more urgent. I must say, if this is the case, they've chosen a fine time to bring the matter up.'

Joanna did not answer for quite a while. She was still feeling slightly sick. 'I really don't know,' she lied. 'But we can't really blame Bernard for this latest development. It appears to have been entirely Felicity's idea.'

'I expect the wretched woman got scared when he fell, thought he might have had a stroke and then simply talked herself into thinking he really had. She's devious, that one. God knows why we're bothering to go out of our way today.'

Joanna began to wonder, too. Although it would be good to have a chance of seeing Mildred and Bertie, what she really wanted to do was to be home on Sunday ready for work the first thing Monday morning. What with having to get up to Hampstead, that would probably not now be possible. And how was she going to explain her sudden visit to Bernard? Would Felicity have primed him as to what she had done?

The afternoon wore on, the countryside around them, flat, uninteresting and shimmering in the heat, the motor road crowded with traffic. Every so often Sam looked at his watch and increased speed. Unlike their original overnight crossing, they were booked on no particular ferry, knowing that one ran almost every twenty minutes on the shorter route. But at Calais there was a hold-up. Queues of angry returning holidaymakers sat in their cars, windows down, transistors blaring. A thunderstorm seemed imminent and, once on the Channel, there was a heavy swell. Joanna felt worse and Sam, disappointed and frustrated, disappeared into the bar.

It was getting quite dark by the time they cleared English customs and were on the road again. There was no doubt, Joanna realised, that they had made the most appalling mistake. They should have gone straight home as planned and she would have made a trip to London some time during the following week. How she had allowed Felicity to bamboozle her into this detour, Joanna had no idea.

Neither did she know what hit them. Whether Sam, used to driving for three weeks on the right-hand side of the road, had simply forgotten he was back in England, whether he was overtired – for she had been feeling too unwell to help out by taking a turn at the wheel – or whether he had drowned his sorrows by indulging too heavily at the bar, were questions which, for the time being, were completely blotted out by a searing pain down her right side, the sound of police cars screaming and the monotonous eerie wail of an ambulance ululating somewhere, so it seemed, just inside her head.

Joanna had no idea that she herself was actually inside the vehicle.

30

Somehow it did not seem all that surprising to wake up and find Mildred sitting by her bed. It was like old times again, comforting and quite in order. She was probably having one of her bronchial spells, Joanna thought.

Then she felt the pain, not in her chest but lower down, in her right side. There appeared to be some kind of contraption hoisting up her leg. And what was this extra-ordinary thing attached to her arm?

A nurse entered the small white room and stood over her, quietly holding her wrist. 'That's fine, Mrs Foster,' she said.

Foster? Why not Lawson? Then it all came back. She was married again. She and Sam had been coming back from their honeymoon. There had been an accident. She recalled the drone of the ambulance. Where was Sam?

'Sam?' she queried Mildred. 'Where's Sam?' The nurse, her head turned away, was making adjustments to the thing on her arm. Mildred remained oddly silent. 'Sam?' Joanna asked again.

She thought the nurse and Mildred seemed to exchange glances. Then Mildred said, 'Sam was badly hurt, Jo.'

'How bad? Is he in the next room?'

Mildred took her hand, thinking of the moving words of the late Canon Scott Holland, which were often quoted at funeral and memorial services, 'I have only slipped away into the next room . . .' How was she to tell Joanna that . . .

Suddenly, violently, Joanna tried to lift herself up. Together, the nurse and Mildred manoeuvred her gently back on to the pillows, while she said, 'Why aren't you answering? You aren't trying to tell me he's dead, are you?'

In the confirming silence, Joanna closed her eyes and Mildred took hold of her hand again, even tighter. No one spoke for what seemed a long time. The nurse left the room. Eventually, still with her eyes closed, Joanna said, 'Where am I?'

'In hospital. At Canterbury.'

'When did you come?'

'Early Sunday morning. Armelle drove me down. She was with me when . . . I heard the news.'

'What day is it today?'

'Tuesday.'

There was a longer silence and Mildred wondered whether perhaps Joanna had dozed off again, until she heard her say, 'Does Bertie know?'

'Yes.'

'And Felicity and Bernard?'

'Yes.'

Mildred did not add that Felicity, trying to absolve herself from any responsibility over bringing the honeymooners back earlier and by another route, had tried to pin all the blame for the accident on Sam, who 'must have been drunk'; nor did Mildred say anything about how she herself was still consumed with guilt for having divulged their whereabouts in the first place; nor that Bertie, according to Mrs Pardoe, was more shocked and distressed than she had ever known him. All she said was, 'Armelle has been wonderful.'

And so sh had, Mildred thought. She had happened to call in late on the Saturday night on her way back from Crane Lodge because she wanted to give Mildred something personally, which had been found by one of the carpenters when he was working earlier that day in Gloria's old bedroom. Much to his excitement and surprise, he had come upon a little cache under one of the loose floor boards near her bed.

Apparently there had been bottles and boxes of every conceivable kind of pill and also countless miniature but mostly empty bottles of spirits, a plastic mug and a long brown sealed envelope. 'I threw all the other stuff away,' Armelle had said, 'but this envelope is addressed to you.'

No sooner had Armelle passed it to Mildred than the telephone rang. It was the Kent police, having found Mildred's name and address from Joanna's diary, reporting the accident. Armelle had then simply taken over. She had given Mildred a stiff brandy out of the bottle – kept for medicinal purposes only – in her wine cupboard. She then went upstairs and threw a few of Mildred's belongings into a hold-all and, with no thought for herself, simply drove straight off into the night with her new charge. The envelope remained on the sitting-room table.

The authorities at the hospital gave Mildred an emergency bed. Armelle snatched a few hours' sleep in one of the waiting-rooms, then drove home with a promise to return within forty-eight hours. Since then, Mildred had spent most of the time by Joanna's bed. She was told that Mrs Foster had a good chance of pulling through, although her right leg was badly broken in two places and that it was probable she would be left a cripple. Her husband had been dead on arrival at the hospital. On hearing of Mildred's long association with the patient, the doctor said he would leave it to her as to when and how to impart this news.

That had now been taken out of Mildred's hands by Joanna herself but, as for the future, the questions seemed too desperate and numerous to contemplate. What would happen to Jo's business? Sam's affairs? Where would Joanna go? Mildred was only too willing to give her a home for as long as was necessary but she was acutely aware of her age and that because neither Joanna nor Sam had ever had children, there was no one of the younger generation who could step in to deal with the practical side of affairs. Bertie was too old and incapacitated. Bernard was simply incapacitated. Felicity was worse than useless. Solicitors, presumably, would do their best.

Then, suddenly and thankfully, Mildred realised that she was reckoning without Armelle.

She had arrived, as promised, two days later, looking refreshed and immaculate as always. It seemed as if emergencies, the need to be needed, were what she thrived on. She stayed the night in a nearby hotel and suggested to Mildred that she would book up for both of them to stay there every weekend until Joanna was fit enough to leave hospital. 'Meanwhile,' she said, 'I think you should come back home, Mildred,' having noticed the all too obvious signs of strain and lack of sleep in the older woman's face.

'Not until I'm sure Joanna's out of danger.'

Armelle was not surprised at the reply. 'All right, stay until next week, when I'm certain she will be. Meanwhile, I thought I'd drive down to the west country and see what's to be done about her shop. I've been in touch with her local solicitor who, fortunately, is the same one as Sam's.' She paused. 'There's all his affairs, too.' She paused. 'His funeral, even. It seems to me someone's got to do something in that direction.'

'Thank you, Armelle.'

It seemed impossible to believe that this woman who had so recently come into their lives, who none of them – except, perhaps Bernard – had particularly taken to, was now so indispensable. It was as if she had been sent. Was there a plan in life, Mildred wondered, and death? How much was Jo's and Sam's accident pre-ordained? No, that was wrongful thinking. It could absolve anyone from any responsibility whatsoever. Nevertheless, Mildred could not help feeling like some pawn, caught up in an extraordinary set of circumstances which had been sparked off by Gloria's death and wasn't finished yet.

It was not until she was home again that Mildred gave any thought to the letter which had been left lying on the sitting-room table on that fateful night when Armelle had driven her straight off to Canterbury. Even now, she waited until her benefactor had left, having ascertained that the provisions they had stopped to buy en route were quite adequate for Mildred to have a reasonable supper.

Then she picked it up and went to sit by the window which looked out, rather as Bertie's did, on to the Thames. The nights were drawing in now and, other things being equal, she had been looking forward to watching the view of the river quietly from her own domain. Now, she simply stared at it, unseeingly, frightened of she knew not what she might find in the still unopened missive in her hand. Why should Gloria write her a letter and then hide it away where no one, other than some strange workman, might come upon it by chance? What did she want with Mildred now, a year after her death? Surely there was nothing more that Mildred could do for her? She had cleared up Crane Lodge, cared for Jason until he died, tried to do her best for Joanna, Bertie, Bernard, Felicity and even little George. Was there still some behest outstanding? Had Gloria imagined that there would always be time to give Mildred the letter personally, or at least tell her where it was? Had she put it off, like so many things, so that there was now only a dead hand stretching out to demand some other duty from the grave?

Mildred's own hand shook a little as she at last summoned up courage to slit the envelope. Even then, she procrastinated a little, while she got up to fetch her glasses. Wearily, she sat back in the chair again. The last few weeks had taken their toll and she was very tired. Presently, with an effort, she began to read *The Last Will and Testament of Gloria Lilian Rayner*. It was dated shortly before her death and witnessed, quite correctly, by the two people in the room with her, Ivy and John Jamieson.

It was perfectly straightforward. There seemed to be no doubt about it at all. Everything the deceased possessed was bequeathed to Mildred Cicely Treadgold, outright, 'in recognition of all she has done for me over a long period of time.'

31

In the fall of that year, a frail elderly lady could be seen walking along the towpath at Strand-on-the-Green. Every so often she paused to rest a little and get her breath, pretending to study a boat going up or down the river, or the swooping screaming seagulls driven inland by the impending gale, taking refuge by the water's edge; for the last thing Mildred ever wanted was to draw attention to herself or admit to a disability which had increasingly afflicted her during recent months.

The shock of discovering that Gloria had made another will – and entirely in her favour – had given Mildred the same funny trembling feeling in her heart which she had first noticed while she had been sitting by Joanna's bed in the hospital. At that time, she had tried to ignore it and, certainly, as Joanna improved, it had seemed to go away; but after she arrived home again to be faced with quite a different kind of anguish, the palpitation, or whatever it was, had returned. Urged by Armelle, who regularly called in to see her and had once found Mildred doing something she had never done for as long as she could remember – spending a day in bed – she had been forced into consulting her doctor.

'Fibrillation,' was the term he used to describe her condition, after giving Mildred a thorough examination which included an electrocardiogram. He had gone on to assure her that many people suffered from the same trouble, especially with advancing years, and although, in all probability, the fibrillation would become permanent, it could always be regulated by adjusting the daily dose of digoxin which he now proposed she should take indefinitely.

He had known Mildred a long time – though rarely as a patient, only as the long-suffering companion to Gloria – and he was aware of all she had recently gone through, particularly the devastating accident to Joanna and Sam. Yet, good doctor that he was, he sensed – rather as Mildred thought Armelle Levitte also seemed to sense – that she was withholding some extra trouble and wondered what it could possibly be. But on trying to probe a little further, he noticed her agitation increase and he let the matter drop. All in good time, perhaps, she would tell him what was on her mind, for he had asked her to visit his surgery regularly every fortnight 'just to keep an eye on you,' he had said, cheerfully, 'and to see the pills are doing the trick.'

Mildred had promised she would do this, but she had no intention of telling him or anyone else that she had just had the opportunity of possibly becoming an immensely rich woman. Such information, far from making her elated, had thrown her into the depths of despair and confusion.

Joanna's accident and Sam's death had been horrendous enough, but the grief Mildred had then suffered and from which she was still suffering was within the bounds of normality. This business of Gloria's other will was unreal, abnormal, something about which she felt quite unable to talk to anyone and which made her appear strange and distrait to those who knew her.

Mildred supposed, according to law, she should show the new will immediately to Hugh Cory. The fact that it was to her own advantage was neither here nor there. That was the letter of the law and Mildred had never broken a law in her life. To withhold this latest discovery, written on an ordinary form obtainable from most stationers, but drawn up and witnessed, obviously correctly, by both Jamiesons at the same time, was tantamount to a criminal act. Yet how could it be criminal to forgo worldly goods in favour of others? She thought, as she so often had, about the evening Ivy and John had called to see Gloria shortly before her death and how odd she had thought their visit to be. She could see it all now. It had been carefully arranged and Gloria, for once, had remained surprisingly sober that evening.

No wonder the Jamiesons imagined that Mildred would be staying on at Crane Lodge. Yet why, if Gloria had meant her to have her entire estate, had she hidden this new will? Was it because she thought she might change her mind and simply tear it up, but right at that moment she was angry with Bernard for never coming to see her and not on altogether too good terms with Joanna and Bertie either?

There were so many other factors in the situation which had just developed that literally made Mildred's head hurt to think of them. Supposing she *did* go to Hugh Cory and produce the document. Would all that had taken place over the past year, all that had been settled and put into operation – at enormous cost and effort – have to be cancelled? (The first long-awaited hand-outs of income were due any moment.) Would she, Mildred, have to finalise things regarding the sale of the archive and Sam's book? There would sure to be talk of Counsel's opinion being sought once more, the whole wearisome business of executing the will dragged up and re-opened, causing untold trouble. Bernard would be more than likely to have a *real* stroke. Felicity would be beside herself; and although Joanna and Bertie would no doubt accept the changed circumstances with equanimity, surely it would be better to leave things as they were and let the four beneficiaries have what they were expecting.

Besides, what good could it possibly do for her, Mildred, to inherit the whole of Gloria's estate? She did not want the money. She had never understood the desire most people seemed to have for it. Over and above a reasonable limit, what did they want it *for*? She was still governed by that old maxim of her mother's: *one's wants may be many, one's needs are few.* And now that she was so much older, Mildred had found that even her modest wants had become fewer and fewer. One could only eat or drink so much a day, wear one set of clothes or occupy one home at a time. She supposed it might be different for some people, especially if they were younger. They could go on shopping sprees, acquire valuable possessions, socialise, travel or, perhaps, if philanthropically inclined, give to charity. Mildred thought if she did find herself the possessor of great wealth she would try to pass most of it on to Joanna, some to Great Ormond Street Hospital for Sick Children and some to her eldest nephew and niece. But not to Rory. She had never been a woman to bear grudges, but somehow she drew the line at her youngest nephew. She did not like him. He had let the side down.

But dear Jo, so tragically bereaved and with probably a permanent disability and the need to sell her business, her case was uppermost in Mildred's mind all the time. It would be nice to give her whatever she could, even if it were only in a material sense. Mildred believed there were ways and means of doing this, but she was not a clever woman and it would necessitate seeking advice and divulging her secret in order to go about it. And, what was even more important, it would take *time*, judging by the fact that it was over a year since Gloria died and no one had actually benefited from it yet, except perhaps the firm of Pemberton Stubbs. Since the business about her heart, Mildred had a nasty feeling that time was not on her side.

With any luck, she thought, Joanna would still outlive them all and Gloria's capital would go where it was most deserved. The girl seemed to be getting better, though slowly, and she was still on crutches. Soon she was due to go to a rehabilitation centre where physiotherapists helped to get people back on their own two feet again. It would be a tragedy if this did not happen and if, for some unaccountable reason, Bernard ended up by winning the jackpot; but even then, Mildred tried to think charitably. He had, after all, been sick.

She walked on slowly towards Kew Bridge, a cold east wind at her back, making her realise that the homeward journey would be that much more difficult to accomplish. She noticed the little barricades against flooding which had been erected at many a front door. It made her think of the coming winter and Christmas. It didn't seem possible that it would soon be upon them all, nor that, contrary to what she had imagined, the one which she had organised a year ago might not be the last which all the beneficiaries would spend at Crane Lodge.

The place was not due to open officially until the following year, but it had been arranged that Bertie should be installed there in the middle of December, Mrs Pardoe's rapidly worsening arthritis making him decide to move as soon as he could before the really cold weather set in. Armelle had intimated that there would also be a room for Joanna by then, if she would like one, and that she hoped she would stay for as long a period of convalescence as she wished, even hinting that she would be very welcome to remain in a kind of managerial capacity at the Rayner Rest Home. Invitations to spend Christmas day there had also been cordially extended to Bernard, Felicity, George and Mildred and the latter had got as far as thinking that if she did take Armelle up on that, then she could wear her new – at least, new to her – grey dress that she had bought for the occasion the previous year; but she had quickly chided herself for such a flippant thought in the midst of so much sadness and other complications. What was a dress when poor Jo was a widow on crutches for whom Christmas at Crane Lodge would bring back far too many painful memories of Sam, and she herself was this very moment intent on breaking the law.

The nearer Mildred got to Kew Bridge, the more guilty she felt. She scuttled past Bertie's front door, not only because she did not want to be seen by him or Mrs Pardoe, but because she felt as if the police were after her. The tide, thank goodness, was high – she had made certain of that – and she took out the little sealed packet, weighted with the head of an old broken hammer, from the pocket of her ten-year-old overcoat.

It was, she knew, really rather ridiculous to be surreptitiously disposing of Gloria's last will in this way. Many had been the time when she had thought simply to tear it up and quietly consign it to one of the refuse collectors' black sacks. But somehow she hadn't been able to bring herself to do it. This morning, however, when she had watched them for what seemed like the hundredth time drive off in their huge all-devouring vehicle without it, she knew it was now or never. The rubbish was not due to be collected for another three days, a lifetime away. She could not wait a moment longer. Fetching the kitchen scissors, Mildred cut the last will and testament of Gloria Lilian Rayner into little pieces and parcelled it up for its last journey.

It had not been all that difficult, Mildred thought afterwards, throwing the packet into the Thames from Kew Bridge. Nobody appeared to be passing at the time. It gave her the most immense satisfaction to see it sink at once. Getting rid of the small weight had lifted a disproportionately heavier weight from her mind. Infinitely relieved, she left the scene of her wrong-doing feeling almost jaunty. It was only when she turned to walk eastwards back the way she had come that the trouble began.

The wind had gained force. She had to struggle against it. Her heart started fluttering about, almost as if she had a caged bird inside her chest. It occurred to her that she might stop and make a call on Bertie. But somehow she did not want to see one of the other beneficiaries so soon after her secretive, unusual and, she felt, underhand act. She must press on. Her own home, her own bed, the desire to lie down and sleep on it, was overwhelming.

Mildred was only two doors away from the new block of flats in which she lived on the second floor, quietly thanking God that she had had the good sense to acquire a place with a lift, when it happened. She found she needed rather a longer pause than usual. In fact, she did not think she could walk a step further, let alone any kind of staircase.

Her body suddenly seemed to crumple up and sank down on to the path, where Mrs Pardoe, passing five minutes later on her way to buy Bertie some lamb cutlets, found her 'all of a heap, like', as she subsequently told the coroner at the inquest, 'every bit of life quite gone out of her body, poor thing.'

32

'Mrs Foster is not seeing visitors at present.' The matron of the rehabilitation centre in East Sussex did not mention that Joanna had told her that there were two people for whom she would always make an exception: Mr Herbert Fane and also a Madame Levitte, who was apparently attending to her business affairs.

'But I am Mrs Foster's only brother,' Bernard persisted, tetchily. He, too, had carefully refrained from mentioning the fact that he was merely a half one. An *only* brother would surely mean much more to the person on the other end of the line, whom he felt to be singularly obstinate and obtuse. 'My wife and I would like to drive down and see her this Sunday. Naturally, we should not stay long. We are well aware of all Mrs Foster has recently been through.'

'Just one moment, please.' The line went dead and Bernard was left hanging on, annoyed that there appeared to be something badly amiss with the inter-communication system of this particular establishment.

After what seemed more like a hundred moments rather than one, the same precise reserved voice – reminding him of the Sister-in-Charge of the Silbury Clinic – said, 'Mrs Foster could see you on Sunday afternoon after 3 pm, but for no longer than a quarter of an hour. She is still far from well and has been greatly set back by a second bereavement. An elderly lady, I understand, who meant much to her.'

'Yes, yes.' Bernard, having got what he wanted – or as good as he felt he was likely to get – was anxious to end the call. 'Our old nannie,' he added, shortly. 'But she was a good age. It was only to be expected.'

Although was it, he wondered, after putting down the receiver. He recalled how he had once described Mildred as the wiry type, likely to go on for ever. Of course, Jo's and Sam's accident must have been a shock to the old girl. He supposed it could have been the cause of heart failure from which she appeared to have died. He had no idea that she was already being treated for such a possibility.

He himself had certainly had a shock – albeit of a different and far less distressing kind – when Bertie had telephoned to tell him of Mildred's demise. It had been a relief when he and Felicity were unable to attend the funeral, because she had a bad cold and he felt sure he was about to go down with one, too. He understood Mildred was against cremation and he didn't fancy the idea, under any circumstances, of standing around in a graveyard at this time of the year. Apparently Mildred had a brother, thank God, who had turned up to take care of everything.

The death of the elderly woman who had devoted so much of her life to him meant, regrettably, little to Bernard, other than to prompt him into renewing his efforts to get Joanna's agreement to breaking the trust once Bertie had passed on. He felt the latter event could hardly be much longer now. It would then be ridiculous for two people of roughly the same age to remain wondering who was going to inherit Gloria's capital outright. Joanna could probably do with a lump sum, now that she might be left semi-incapacitated. He wasn't against her having half. That was only fair under the present circumstances. Besides, if he played his cards right and she happened to pop off before him, he could easily find he was a beneficiary of her own will or, at any rate, George. After all, she was a widow with no dependants and had always seemed quite fond of his stepson.

The following Sunday, therefore, Bernard set off for Sussex, with Felicity driving, feeling reasonably pleased with life. Things, on the whole, were working out. He had not had a drink for six months. Soon, all being well, he would get his licence back. On the rear seat of the BMW there was not only a huge arrangement of chrysanthemums and carnations, but also several new biographies, which he thought his half-sister would enjoy. He was incapable of appreciating that Joanna, in her present condition, could scarcely be expected to enjoy anything.

At exactly ten past three, after lunching at a nearby road-house, Bernard and Felicity stood in the doorway of Joanna's room, all smiles and armed with gifts, presenting to anyone unacquainted with the family history a perfect picture of kindred love and affability. That this seemed to have little effect on the person they had come to see was, perhaps, somewhat daunting, but Bernard was in no way prepared to be deflected from the main purpose of his visit. He sat down on one of the hard upright chairs, Felicity took the only easy one in the corner and his half-sister, fully clothed, remained lying on her bed.

'My dear Jo.' The patient's quietness and lack of response was something which Bernard was determined to overcome. 'We've been so desperately sorry about . . . all that happened.'

'Yes?' The word was framed as a question, dispassionate, uninterested.

'I do want you to feel . . .' Bernard said, beginning to lose a little of his initial confidence and bonhomie, 'that Felicity and I want to do all that is in our power to help.'

'Thank you,' Joanna replied in the small silence which seemed to have descended on the room like a temporary numbing, a lull before some louder verbal contretemps took place.

'I mean . . . we realise how . . .' Bernard had definitely begun to flounder now, searching for the correct adjective and unfortunately came out with '*bloody* everything has been for you.' He had never been noted for his sensitivity in expressing himself. 'You would be most welcome to stay with us after leaving here,' he went on, hurriedly, and then came to a full stop.

'Thank you, but I have already made arrangements,' came the same quiet unenthusiastic response. Bernard had discussed this invitation with Felicity and both knew that it was quite safe to extend it. Joanna would never come to Hampstead.

Worried that time was passing, he continued, rather desperately, 'But whatever happens, Jo, I feel that eventually you may well need a very special kind of home. I mean, let's hope it won't be necessary, but you might want to buy some place with every convenience, every mod. con., so to speak. Every luxury, indeed. You deserve it.' That last was a good touch, he felt. Warming to his theme,

Bernard went on, 'And speaking of that, I do feel that once you and I are the only two beneficiaries left in Ma's will, we ought to get Hugh Cory to see about breaking the trust. After all, old Pemberton said we could have done that in the beginning, except that *quartering* the capital simply wasn't on, to my way of thinking. But *halving* it between you and me, well, that's a different matter altogether. I'm sure you'll see the sense of that.'

Felicity, who had been staring out of the window, watching some patients on crutches moving awkwardly about in the garden below, now turned towards her sister-in-law. She had been going to say something in support of her husband's proposition, but the look on Joanna's face made her hold back, the words sticking on the tip of her tongue like some nasty taste.

An unnatural flush now seemed to suffuse Joanna's whole countenance. A hardness came into her normally gentle eyes. With the aid of a stick, she struggled off the bed and stood up, her voice, when she spoke, no longer quiet, nor apathetic.

'What you are asking me, Bernard,' she replied, 'is to anticipate my father's death, agree to some mercenary deal to take place after it, an event which would no doubt suit you down to the ground. I must ask if you would both now please go and leave me alone.'

Startled and discomfited, Felicity and Bernard felt they could do no more than she asked. Joanna waited until the door closed behind them. Then she lay back on her bed, exhausted. The cost – especially in her weakened state – of facing the issue in such a bold, hostile and uncharacteristic fashion, had been considerable.

'It would have been better,' Felicity said, as soon as they were in the car again, 'if you'd waited a little longer.' The sight of the patients which she had witnessed that afternoon and the guilt which she had all along been trying to suppress over the part she had so tragically played in connection with Joanna's disabilities had at last caught up with her.

'I don't agree,' Bernard, thwarted and angry, was determined to vindicate his actions. 'Jo was always difficult.

Too damned independent. Wanting her own way. It's obvious all that side of her is getting worse. The accident could well have affected her judgement.'

'She didn't strike me as having any trouble in that direction. After all, she *has* had a raw deal, Bernard. I couldn't help feeling sorry for her, in spite of the way she dismissed us. She was looking far worse than I expected, especially at the end. Did you notice how much she was shaking?'

'She was worked up. She didn't realise I was trying to do her a good turn.'

Felicity was silent. She knew it was no use arguing with Bernard in this mood. The light was fading and she never liked driving at the best of times. She merely let him rumble on, intermittently, all the way to Hampstead.

It was about half past nine that evening when the telephone rang. Bernard answered it and found himself being addressed by the same woman to whom he had spoken earlier in the week although, this time, her voice seemed even quieter and more reserved.

'Mr Rayner?'

'Speaking.'

'I am so very sorry. I am afraid I have bad news . . . Your sister . . . Mrs Foster, suffered a fatal stroke a few hours after you left today. I have already notified Mr Herbert Fane, whom she named as next of kin.'

Shortly after midnight when Felicity, unable to sleep, came downstairs to find out why Bernard had not come up to bed, she discovered him, together with an almost empty bottle of whisky, stretched out on the floor of his study.

33

One autumnal afternoon several years later, a smart red sports car turned in at the entrance to the Rayner Rest Home, raced up the drive and came to a halt by the wide glass-plated front door. The driver had come to pay a duty call on his mother who was a resident, but the person whom he most looked forward to seeing on these occasions was the owner of the place, Madame Levitte.

George Rayner had developed into a tall thin serious-looking young man with a shy diffident charm. He was now up at Oxford reading history. His stepfather had been dead for some time and George had been given to understand that when he was twenty-five he would come into quite a considerable fortune from a trust fund set up on his behalf by Bernard Rayner before his death, in which his wife, Felicity, had a life interest.

George had not really paid a lot of attention to the matter until lately. At public school – where he had done exceptionally well – he had been too busy concentrating on matters in hand: being a house prefect, head of the debating society, deputy editor of the magazine, and, finally, to everyone's surprise including his own, coming first in the annual cross-country run.

George had been in the Upper Fifth when Bernard had died of cirrhosis of the liver, his lapses into alcoholism becoming more frequent towards the end. George had returned home for the funeral and was surprised to discover his mother so distracted and tearful. As a child, he had never noticed Bernard and Felicity showing much affection towards one another. Indeed, they had always seemed at loggerheads. But, now, Bernard's widow was full of protestations of love for her late husband and seeming remorse for not having taken more care of him. She kept clinging on to George and saying he was all she had, something which the boy found both distasteful and embarrassing.

Bernard's lawyer – the last of many whom he had consulted over the years – had taken great pains to explain to

George the will which Bernard had finally made – at Felicity's instigation – when he had found himself the sole surviving beneficiary under the terms of another will: that of the late Gloria Lilian Rayner. It suddenly began to dawn on George that he and his mother were very lucky to have been left so well provided for. Nevertheless, he did wish Felicity wouldn't carry on so much concerning two things about which he knew very little: love and money. Ever since his step-grandmother had died, Felicity and Bernard had seemed to do nothing else but argue about the latter – he always remembered a particularly unfortunate outing when he was at prep school, and the two of them had gone on and on about wills and trusts and legacies, and speculating on how long an old girl called Mildred, and another even more shadowy figure called Bertie, might live. It had always shocked George that they appeared to wish them both dead.

After his stepfather had died, George hoped that all this kind of thing was at an end. But it seemed as if this was not to be. During the school holidays, Felicity kept harping on the subject until George seriously began to wonder whether his mother was quite right in the head. He often felt she had something on her mind, but whenever he tried to find out what it was she went off on a tangent.

One Easter holiday, when he was in his last year at school, her doctor had taken him aside and said that he felt Felicity should go into some residential establishment where she would receive expert care, rather than continue at Hampstead with the housekeeper/companions who came and went with extraordinary rapidity, none of them being able to cope with the vagaries of their employer for very long. He went on to explain to George that although his mother was not yet sixty, some people aged more quickly than others, and while he did not actually mention the word, the boy was astute enough to know that he was referring to the very same complaint from which Felicity had often alleged Bernard was suffering: Alzheimer's Disease.

George had immediately thought of the Rayner Rest Home and had gone to see Armelle, who had always done her best to maintain contact with her half-brother's widow and child. For the sake of the family, as she put it, she was willing to accommodate Felicity, although well aware that her case would not be an easy one. She also kindly suggested that, should he need it, there would always be a small room available for George during the holidays.

Surprisingly – or perhaps not so surprisingly, considering she had never been much of a home-maker – Felicity raised no objection to the move, as long as she could have one of the best suites. And here it was, in the self-same bedroom and sitting-room once personally occupied by her late mother-in-law, that Felicity Rayner, growing more and more confused and forgetful, came to pass her days. In some curious way, she now seemed to bear a striking resemblance to Gloria, so much so that although George had seen comparatively little of his late step-grandmother, he remembered enough about her to make him suspect that she was the reason why Bernard had married his mother, men often being attracted to maternal look-alikes.

It upset George to watch his own mother going downhill, not to be able to hold a reasonable conversation with her or to do anything about her condition. Frustrated, he tried to think of a reason why she had gone the way she had, and wondered whether there had been some initial shock or worry that had triggered it off. The two of them had never been close but he was her only son, the only person, in fact, whom she seemed to have in the world, for she had never been a woman to make, let alone keep, any friends.

On this particular occasion, after he had said goodbye to her before driving on to London, where he now had a small flat acquired as a base when he had attained the age of eighteen, he had gone in search, as he invariably did, of Armelle. He was not in quite so much awe of her these days. He felt that she liked him and he admired the way she always looked so *soignée* and the fact that she seemed to have so much savoir-faire. Today she gave him tea – a proper tea instead of the one he had just had with his mother – for Armelle knew that he had not yet outgrown his love of buttered toast and chocolate cake. After the first few mouthfuls, he came straight to the point.

'Armelle, I want to ask you something.' (He had now, after much persuasion, got around to using her Christian name.) 'Have you ever thought my mother has, or at any rate used to have because she's so vague these days, something on her mind?'

'*Mais oui*. Frequently.'

'Have you any idea what it is – or was?'

The Frenchwoman looked at him. 'Perhaps.'

'Then, please, I should like to know. I don't suppose it will do any good now, but it all seemed so odd after my stepfather died, the way she went to pieces. How she kept harping on about money and the four beneficiaries and Bernard outliving them all and scooping the pool, so to speak. How I've come to hate the word beneficiary.'

Armelle Levitte smiled. 'Yes, I can understand how you feel.'

'Then what exactly happened?'

'I've never known everything, you understand. But I have a good idea. Money, my dear George, is a very powerful thing, almost, but not quite, as powerful as sex. Some people, very few, know how to handle it. Your step-grandmother in her early days was an extravagant woman, but as she got older she . . . how do you say in England? . . . drew in her horns. She died a rich woman but unfortunately she made one highly controversial will.'

'What do you mean by one?'

'I'll come to that later. As you know, she left her estate, or rather the income from it, to be divided equally between her son, her daughter, Bertie Fane and Mildred Tread-gold. The last survivor, who happened to be your step-father, was to inherit the capital outright. Mildred was the first to die from heart failure. Joanna, who was the victim of a car crash, died not long afterwards at a special hospital for rehabilitating such victims. Bertie Fane, who came to live here for a short time, simply faded away. By then he had nothing left to live for. He was Joanna's father.'

'*Was* he now? I never knew. Please go on.'

'Well, as he was no real relation of yours, I think I can safely call your stepfather an avaricious man. I'm afraid your mother encouraged him in this, but . . .' Armelle hesitated and then went on, kindly, 'I think she was probably motivated because she had you to think of.'

'Oh, God.'

'Anyway, between them, Felicity and Bernard were anxious that none of Gloria's capital should go to Mildred or Bertie who were, after all, both getting on. I believe Bernard was biding his time until both of them had passed away and then he hoped to come to some arrangement with Joanna, whereby they broke the trust and split the capital fifty fifty. With a clever lawyer it would probably have been possible. When Joanna married, rather unexpectedly, they were even more anxious to get her agreement to this idea. Felicity even dragged her and her husband back early from their honeymoon, because she thought Bernard was ill and she wanted to get the matter settled once and for all. I don't suppose you were aware of any of this. I believe you were away spending the summer holidays with friends.'

'Yes. I remember hearing about the smash. I thought Jo died from it. I was sorry, because I liked her.'

'No, it was Sam who was killed instantly. Joanna was sent to this hospital I mentioned, where Felicity and Bernard went to see her. By then, they couldn't leave well alone. They were like a dog with a bone, I suppose. Even though Bertie was still on the scene, Bernard wanted some kind of promise out of Jo. Naturally, she would have been very upset. She'd only recently been twice bereaved and was in pain, mentally and physically. I imagine there was an almighty row. The idea of planning something for after Bertie's death was totally repugnant to her. After all, he was her father. Within a few hours of their visit, she had a fatal stroke.'

'So that just left Bernard and Bertie?'

'Yes. Bertie never got over Jo's death. As I said, he came here for a time, but I could tell it would not be a long one.

I don't know how much he knew about the real reason for his daughter's death.'

'But how did *you* know?'

Armelle held out her hand for his cup and refilled it before she continued, 'When your mother first came here she sometimes confided in me, in a roundabout kind of way. She might often have seemed grasping and impossible, but she was a very insecure person, very dependent on your stepfather. I began to feel sorry for her. She needed, how shall I put it, direction as well as protection. You will often find that those who are emotionally insecure need to surround themselves with the outward trappings of security: wealth, possessions, husbands or wives, as the case might be. By now, although she had acquired the financial security she had been hankering after, she started regretting the way it had been obtained. She was not without a conscience, George. I think she felt that she and Bernard had killed off Jo and, indirectly, Mildred and Bertie. After all, the honeymooners would probably be alive today if they had stuck to their original plans for their homecoming, and it was almost criminal to go and bother Joanna about Gloria's will so soon after her bereavements and accident. I believe that these two impulsive and insensitive acts, resulting in Bernard inheriting Gloria's whole estate, began to haunt her.'

There was silence in the room now, the same room and at the same time of year where once, many years ago all four beneficiaries had sat along with Percy Pemberton and Hugh Cory to hear how Gloria had bequeathed her estate. George looked out of the window. The evening light had begun to cast long shadows on the well-kept lawns and cheerful colourful flower-beds, scarlet and yellow dahlias mingling with mauve michaelmas daisies. Soon, George knew he must be on his way. There was a girl he was meeting at his flat at six o'clock. But what Armelle had just told him had, for the moment, pushed all thought of the forthcoming evening out of his mind. He turned to his hostess.

'You said you were coming to something else. You mentioned there was one will. Was there a later one?'

Mentally, Armelle Levitte applauded him for his quickness, his grasp of the situation.

'Yes.'

'Who knows about it? What happened? Was it never produced?'

'I am the only person who knows about it, George, apart from the two witnesses, both of whom have long since died. I have no idea what happened to it. Only that I suspect it was destroyed.'

'By whom?'

'By Mildred Treadgold.'

'*Mildred Treadgold?* But she was the soul of righteousness, wasn't she?'

'Yes. Of course she was.'

'Then I don't understand.'

'The will was entirely in her favour. Gloria left her everything outright. The envelope was addressed to her and discovered by a workman when I was having this place renovated. He gave it to me and I gave it to Mildred. I think it caused her untold anguish. By then, the first will had been all but executed.'

'Did she tell you about it?'

'No, George. She kept the secret to herself. But the envelope was not particularly well stuck up. From its size and shape, I guessed what it might be. Anyway, I was curious. I looked at it before passing it over. I had no business to do so, but then, I fear I am no saint.'

He was silent for a long time. A maid came in and removed the tea things. Somewhere at the back of the house someone was playing Tchaikovsky on a piano.

Presently, he said, 'I really have no right to all this money, have I? What the hell am I going to do with it?'

Armelle Levitte smiled again. 'You have plenty of time to decide. I have a feeling you will put it to good use. In the hands of the right person, money can do a great deal of good. It doesn't necessarily produce all the problems such as I have been describing.'

He looked at his watch and got up to go.

'Thank you for telling me all this – and for the tea.'

'It's been a pleasure. Come again soon.'

She watched the little sports car disappear down the drive and sighed, wishing, not for the first time, that she had had children of her own. As one got older it was good to have an interest in the younger generation, watch them grow up, see how they turned out. Like Mildred had so often done, she reflected on the extent to which genes or upbringing affected an individual's charater. George had certainly had a pretty raw deal from the point of view of his upbringing, but he seemed amazingly well adjusted in spite of it. She wondered whether his father had really been as bad as Felicity and Bernard had made out. It was difficult not to believe there must have been some good in him somewhere. She was sorry that the boy's efforts to trace him had only resulted in discovering he was dead. Of course, there was always another possibility concerning George's paternity, one which Armelle kept to herself. But the idea had taken hold after Felicity, in one of her more lucid moments, had said something about her first husband being the jealous type. Had she had some kind of fling? Was that why she was divorced? Why George's so-called father had pushed off and appeared to have denied any responsibility for the child? That could be another reason for Felicity's guilt. Armelle would never know. No one would ever know now. Better not to think about it, let alone talk about it. She had already done quite enough talking for one afternoon, had kept George far too long from what she was sure was an important date.

But although he was a little late arriving at his flat, George was not unduly worried. He knew Caroline had a spare key. He let himself in and found her sitting on the floor, reading a book out of one of his bookshelves. He knelt down and kissed the top of her head.

'I didn't know,' she said, 'that you were interested in cannibals and jungles and all that kind of thing.'

'I'm not,' he replied, giving her another kiss. The book slid on to the carpet, open at the title page, facing a photograph of a young Sir Reginald Rayner standing beside an African chief.

'Was he,' Caroline asked, a little later, 'some sort of ancestor of yours?'

'Not the chief,' George replied, smiling. 'Neither of them were blood relations. But I suppose you could say that, indirectly, thanks to the Rayner chap, I'm here in this flat today. Tell me, where would you like to go for dinner?'